The Metamorphosis of Emma Murry

Rebecca Laxton

Illustrations by Gracie Laxton

This is a work of fiction. Names, characters, businesses, places, events, locales, and incidents are either the products of the author's imagination or used in a fictitious manner.

Copyright © 2023 by Rebecca Laxton

All rights reserved. This book may not be reproduced or stored in whole or in part by any means without the written permission of the author except for brief quotations for the purpose of review.

ISBN: 978-1-960146-22-9 hard cover
       978-1-960146-23-6 soft cover
Laxton. Rebecca.
The Metamorphosis of Emma Murry.

Edited by: Melissa Long

Published by Warren Publishing
Charlotte, NC
www.warrenpublishing.net
Printed in the United States

*For: Steve,
Mikaela, Carleigh,
Gracie, and Jacob
such luck, to be
surrounded by
so much
love*

.

Chapter 1

Sketchbook definitions:
Color: light reflected off objects.

Sophie and I sat in the sky surrounded by the inky twilight. We were perched on the edge of Paul's Peak, way above the town of Black Mountain, closer to Jupiter and the moon than to my family's hardware store. At least, it seemed that way.

We waited for the sunrise. It didn't disappoint.

It started with orange-red burning low along the tops of the hazy mountains. Then, the sun crept up in a circle of fiery orange. Its flames climbed higher and higher in an explosion of orange so bright, the wispy magenta clouds couldn't hold it back. Streaks of light shot down the tops of the trees all the way to the town sleeping in the valley.

Sophie jumped up and pointed toward the sun. "Please, observe the powerful dwarf star," she said, imitating our favorite science teacher, Mrs. Watson, "made up of hydrogen and helium, that holds our solar system together, warms our planet—"

"And colors the morning sky by scattering orange and yellow wavelengths through the atmosphere," I added.

"—but most importantly, KEEPS EVERY LIVING THING ALIVE!" Sophie raised her arms toward the sun as shades of orange spilled across the mountains like hot lava oozing out of a volcano.

We glowed in orange-red hues—a part of the mountain, the sky, the sunrise. My favorite colors. I wanted to paint them all, but this one was hard to mix. I kept getting it too red. I dipped my watercolor brush pen into the yellow and added a little more to the paint in my mixing tray.

"I forgot how bright it was." Sophie held up her phone and snapped a picture.

"Don't look right at it."

"Geez, Emma, I'm not an idiot. My eyes are closed."

It'd been a while since we'd taken a sunrise hike. When we were little, our dads would piggyback us up the trail so we wouldn't trip over the tree roots and rocks in the dark. We'd sit at the top of the mountain, eating dry Cheerios and drinking from a juice pouch.

Sophie snapped another picture.

"How are you taking pictures if your eyes are closed?"

She moved closer and snapped a selfie with me. "It's almost seven fifteen. We should go," she said as she slid her phone into her back pocket. "It'll take us twenty minutes to hike back to your house to get our skateboards and ten minutes to skate to the monarch butterfly garden. If we don't leave right this second, we'll be late."

"Move. I'm almost done." I shooed her out of the way with my paintbrush. "I can't get the shade right. See how it fades from gold to tangerine? I'm trying to get the color right in between." I added two dots of yellow into my mix.

Sophie stepped out of the way, sighing dramatically. "Mr. Zauber's probably already there."

"Mr. Zauber will be happy to see us whenever. You think anyone else will be showing up this summer?" I squeezed a little water out of the brush pen to clean it and swirled in a little more red. "I bet it'll just be you and me until school starts."

Sophie rocked back and forth. "Orange is orange. It looks great. Let's *go*." With her hands on her hips and auburn hair flitting around her, she looked like a dragonfly about to take flight off the mountain.

She knew it was pointless to rush me. Orange was not just orange. It could be any shade from honey to apricot to tangerine or even orange-pink like coral, peach, and salmon or red-orange like crimson or scarlet. The color I was trying to mix was like orange in the middle of a flame.

One more dot of yellow and a little more water and ... no, not it. Ugh.

"Seriously, Emma."

I swirled a little more red around in the tray and—*wabam*! Perfect match! I filled in the last white spot on the page, blended the colors, and it was done.

I set my sketchbook beside me and stretched, breathing in the warm feeling of catching the perfect moment in time. It was a quick celebration. Sophie clicked my watercolors closed and stuffed them in my backpack.

"Geez. Relax. I'm coming." I stood and brushed the prickly pine needles off my butt, then picked up my sketchbook before she could touch it. My painting was still wet. I held it way out in front of me with my left hand while I packed my brush and mixing tray.

If Sophie were a color, she'd be a crimson red—bright but a little dark, peppy but also grumpy, confident but sometimes bossy. She always wanted to be early. For her, being on time meant you were late.

I was more about getting there whenever. We always fought about it.

It'd always been this way. Since our dads were lifelong best friends—true BFFs—Sophie and I were too. She surprised everyone by being born two weeks early. I was born two weeks late. It worked out great, though, because our birthdays were in the same week in May. We'd just had a huge blowout for our thirteenth. The whole Black Mountain Middle School Environmental Club came. Instead of presents, we asked for plants for the community monarch butterfly garden on the Black Mountain Greenway.

We should've asked for help planting them.

I took a granola bar out before I wiggled into my backpack. Then, I followed Sophie down the trail off Paul's Peak to the shortcut. We didn't usually take the shortcut since it was so close to the Coopers' barn, but the other trail was a lot longer, and Sophie was in a hurry. It really didn't matter anyway because nobody'd lived on the farm since Mr. Cooper died last year. We wouldn't be bothering anyone.

I breathed in the smell of pine trees and summer freedom. Birds serenaded us while the pines swished and oaks' leaves danced. The sun flickered through the trees, making little circles of warm butterscotch light flash at our feet.

A wolf howled.

Wait … not a wolf. There weren't any wolves here. A coyote maybe?

Sophie stopped, and I bumped into her, dropping my half-eaten granola bar and almost smearing my sunrise painting all over her T-shirt.

"Did you hear that?" She pulled her phone out of her pocket and slid the photo screen to video.

"What was it?" I picked the granola bar up off the ground. Pieces of dry leaves and dirt stuck to it.

"A red wolf! It had to be." Sophie's eyes were bright and excited. She'd forgotten all about her hustle to the garden.

We froze on the trail, but all we could hear were birds singing and the wind whooshing through the woods.

"It sounded like it was up ahead." Sophie held her phone in front of her and pushed through the trees. I crushed the granola bar into little pieces for the birds and dropped them as I followed her.

The woods thinned out when we reached the path that led to the Coopers' farm. The barn sat to our left. A layer of fog surrounded it and swept around the headstones in the family graveyard. My body tingled like it had last Halloween when Sophie's older brother, Zac, convinced us to take the Black Mountain ghost tour. He'd grabbed my shoulder when the guide told us about the crooked-neck ghost who haunted the fountain in the town square. I'd jumped right out of my skin.

It howled again.

Sophie lifted her phone and spun in a slow circle. "Where is it coming from?"

Something moved in the barn window. Not a wolf but a long, lean, shadowy figure. But it couldn't be. No one lived there.

"Something's in the barn," I whispered.

"Where?"

"In the window."

"The wolf?"

"No."

The shadowy figure floated back and forth in the window. It looked like … surely wasn't, but it looked like … a ghost. My heart beat right out of my chest.

"There," I gasped, pointing through the trees. "You see it?"

A deep voice echoed across the graves. "Get out!"

"Let's go." I pushed Sophie in the back.

We sprinted away from the graveyard toward the fence that divided the Coopers from the Zaubers. We tore through the trees, jumping over fallen limbs and dodging big branches but running right through the little ones. They stung my arms and legs. My backpack bounced and thumped hard against my back, and my whole body felt like it might explode.

We didn't slow down until we got to my front porch. I set my sketchbook down and put my hands on my knees, huffing in and out, loud and hard. "What was that?" I tried to spit out in between breaths, but the words were all jumbled. My whole body still tingled as I collapsed down on the wooden steps.

Sophie's face was bright red, and her eyes had a wide, glazed-over look.

"What was in the barn?" I asked again when I could finally breathe. I knew the answer, but I wanted to hear her say it. She didn't believe in ghosts. She'd laughed during the whole ghost tour last year. But she *had* to believe now.

She sat next to me and played the video back on her phone. We heard our fast breathing and saw the rush of leaves and grass whizz by, but the phone hadn't picked up the howling, the voice yelling, or the ghost in the window.

"That sucks," Sophie said. "I wanted proof. I can't believe there's a red wolf on Paul's Peak."

"You think that was a red wolf in the barn? It didn't look like a red wolf at all." My heart still thumped like I was running the hundred-meter dash. The video had sent me back into a tailspin of fear.

"Not in the barn. The howling came from the other direction." Sophie typed quickly into her phone. "Listen to this: 'The Fish and Wildlife Service reports the total number of red wolves in the wild to be fewer than twenty-five, all found on the Albemarle Peninsula in North Carolina. Red wolves are now the most endangered canine in the world and one of the rarest mammals.'" Her face lit up like the bright Carolina blue sky shining above her. "And *we* found one! We have to sneak back and get evidence to let them know."

Oh, no. There was no way I was going back there. Sophie didn't believe in ghosts, but I did. "How would a red wolf have gotten all the way here? We're miles away from the Albemarle Peninsula," I asked, trying to keep my voice steady and cool. "Maybe we heard a coyote?" I pulled out my phone and searched "coyote howling." I turned up the volume, and Sophie and I leaned in. It wasn't the same. The howl we heard was deeper and longer.

"It has to be a red wolf," Sophie said as she stood. "It's the only logical explanation."

"Hold on." I pulled my extra hair tie off my wrist and flipped my head upside down to redo my ponytail. I'd run so hard, my other one had flown off somewhere on the Coopers' property. "Are you just gonna ignore what we saw in the barn window?" I flipped back up and looped my hair through the tie.

"I didn't see anything." Sophie swayed impatiently back and forth in her dragonfly pose.

"Then why did you run?"

"Because you said *you* saw somebody. I didn't want to get in trouble for being at the Coopers'."

"I said some*thing* was in the window, not some*body*."

"Whatever." She studied my face. "Wait. You think you saw a ghost? Seriously?"

I shrugged.

"Geez, Emma." Sophie's face looked like my mom's when I left my skateboard in the kitchen. "Like your dad and I keep telling you, those ghost stories in town are made up for the tourists." She sounded like Mom too. Sometimes she could be so annoying.

"They're not." My voice came out louder than I'd meant it to. I took a breath and lowered it. "Eloise McCoy, a.k.a. the little ghost of 1865, struck our store again yesterday. I found the dolls from the dollhouse display hidden all around, staring at me with their creepy doll eyes. One on top of the candy shelf, two in the wheelbarrows in the garden area, one stuck in a postcard slot, and one went completely missing." Just thinking about it made little goosebumps pop up on my arms.

"That's nothing. Some kid must've done it. Seriously, how can you be vice president of the Environmental Club if you believe all that stupid supernatural stuff? We're a fact-based organization. There's no scientific proof ghosts—"

"I just told you the proof about Eloise, and I just saw a ghost in the Coopers' barn. With. My. Own. Eyes. It was long and dark, and it sort of floated back and forth across the window. That's all the proof I need."

Sophie shook her head slowly and sighed, as if I were a dumb little kid afraid of monsters in my closet. "Let's go. Mr. Zauber's waiting for us. I don't want him to have to unload all our plants by himself." She leaned down to pack up my stuff. "Oh, no," she said, frowning. "Your summer project."

My sunrise watercolor was ruined. Some of the branches had smacked it, leaving lines across the page. The colors were smeared. All that work for nothing. I deflated on the porch steps.

"It's still amazing." Sophie picked it up. "Like abstract art. Who's that guy you like? Jackson Pollen?"

"Pollock. It looks nothing like that."

"What's the project?"

"Mrs. Hartford wants us to create fourteen pieces of artwork to demonstrate some of the elements and principles of art. This was *color*. I've got all month, but I wanna get as many done as I can before our class on Saturday."

Sophie flipped it around in different directions. "Yeah. Jackson Pollock. It'll still work. Smear it some more and add some colorful squiggles."

I laughed and took my sketchbook from her. "You know nothing about art."

She laughed too. "True." She hopped off the stairs and started down the walkway. "But I know about science. Let's go back to the Peak after we finish working in the garden. We can prove two things." She turned to face me and held up a finger. "One, there's a red wolf living in the woods and two," she added, holding up another finger, "there's no ghost in the barn."

"Fine. I'll go back to look for evidence of the red wolf, but I'm not going anywhere near that haunted barn."

"You're impossible," she said as she rolled my skateboard out from under the bushes and pushed it toward me.

I stopped my board with my foot. Sophie was being impossible, not me. The question wasn't *if* there was a ghost at the Coopers' but *why*. Why now?

Chapter 2

Intensity: how bright or dull the color is

Sophie and I hopped on our skateboards and coasted out of my driveway onto the blacktop. We'd both crashed a bunch of times last summer, but by fall, we could fly down the greenway all the way to town. Our longboards were built for speed, and we were fast. Once, my fitness tracker app clocked us at nine miles an hour.

Bending my knees, I leaned into the turn on the paved part of the greenway trail and kicked the tail of the board down to jump over the curb. That was the only trick I could do. I really wanted to land an ollie, but I couldn't get any air under the board unless I jumped over something.

We caught up to Mr. Zauber driving his little green utility vehicle. He slowed down when he saw us, easing the UTV to a soft stop so he wouldn't knock over the flowers crammed into the small truck bed.

He tipped his straw hat. "Good morning, Madam President and Madam Vice President. Where is the rest of your environmental club?"

"Probably sleeping," I said.

"Ahh. I remember those lazy summer days of childhood. But I was more like you than your friends." He grinned. "Why do lightning bugs get As in school?"

Sophie and I smiled and shrugged.

"They're very bright," he said, laughing. "Hop on, my little lightning bugs! It's a beautiful day to garden!"

Sophie and I laughed too while we wedged our skateboards into the truck bed next to the flowers. She climbed into the passenger side and scooted across the vinyl bench seat so I could squeeze in next to her.

Mr. Zauber's childhood days were decades ago. He was so old, nobody knew exactly how old he was. My dad said he'd always been old, even before they built the greenway, and Dad and Sophie's dad, Max, used to race their bikes to town down Black Mountain Highway. He dressed old too—plaid bowtie and white leather tennis shoes that he polished white to keep looking new. He looked like he was on his way to a garden tea party, not to plant flowers in a garden.

"Hang on, girls!" he said as he held his hat and gave the UTV some gas. He smiled and his whole face crinkled.

I gripped my backpack with my knees and grabbed onto the handle on the roll bar as the UTV rocketed forward. The plants in the back rattled.

We flew around the corner with our hair blowing in the wind. From a distance, the monarch butterfly garden looked like a colorful impressionist painting. There were spots of orange, puffs of pale blue, blurry patches of bright pink, streaks of violet, dots of yellow, and huge splashes of magenta all along the greenway. As we got closer, the scent of the flowers hit us in waves, swirling and mixing into a jumble of sweetness that made me lightheaded and happy.

Mr. Zauber stopped the UTV when we got to the section our environmental club had started. We planted a bunch of milkweed in early spring, and it had already grown.

"Let's put the two bee balm bushes in the back and the coneflowers on the side with the milkweed," Mr. Zauber said. "We'll put the blanket flowers in the front middle and the sweet alyssum on the sides. It'll be a nice border for this part of the greenway trail and will flow well with the rest of the monarch butterfly garden. Our pollinator friends will appreciate it too." He chuckled.

"Perfect!" Sophie clapped her hands in front of her and held them like she was praying.

I couldn't wait to paint it. "It'll be a living piece of artwork." I smiled at Mr. Zauber.

He smiled back as he handed me and Sophie each a pair of gloves and a shovel. "All right my little lightning bugs. Let's get to work. Ready … set … glow!"

Sophie and I looked at each other and laughed while we put on the gloves. He was the only person who could call us bugs without it sounding insulting.

We got busy digging the holes for the bee balm bushes while Mr. Zauber set the other plants where they should go. He muttered to himself while he worked.

I pushed down hard on the shovel and scooped out the red dirt over and over. After a few minutes, I could feel little beads of sweat ball up on my forehead. It was going to be a long morning, but it'd be totally worth it.

"Looks like you girls have it under control here," Mr. Zauber said as he set the last plant into place. "I'm going to head down the greenway and count the butterfly larva. Last week, I counted two hundred eggs and forty caterpillars. That's up from this time last year. We're making progress!"

"That's awesome!" I said. "Maybe it'll be a record year. I really hope they'll be able to keep monarchs off of the endangered species list."

He shook his head. "It's going to take a lot of effort by a whole lot of people to achieve that, I'm afraid. But I'm very thankful you girls are doing your part." He smiled at us like a proud granddad. "Keep up the good work. I'll come back and check on you later."

"Hey, Mr. Zauber," Sophie said. "Speaking of endangered species, have you ever heard a wolf at the Coopers' property?"

He quit smiling and stared at Sophie. "No. Why?"

"We thought we heard one this morning on the way here."

"Stay off the Coopers' property." He sounded threatening.

"Uh … okay, we will. It's just that they're almost extinct, and if there's one out there, we should let the Environmental Protection Agency know—"

"There're no red wolves around here," he growled. "You are mistaken."

Sophie took a step back, the color draining from her face. Mr. Zauber had never talked to us that way before. He was usually sunny and cheerful like a corny old granddad. If he were a color, he'd be buttery yellow.

He climbed back in the UTV and sped off down the greenway trail.

"That was weird." I pulled off my gloves and wiped the sweat from my forehead.

Sophie stood, stunned in the middle of the flowers, and watched the UTV until it disappeared around the corner. She turned toward me slowly, eyes wide. "Why would he care if we took the shortcut by the barn? I mean, I guess he's right, but still … I've never seen him that mad."

"He couldn't have been mad about that. How would he have known?"

"Maybe he saw us. Maybe it was him in the barn."

Ugh. The barn. Coldness washed over me as I pictured the floating figure in the window. I shook my head to clear away the scary vision. "No. That definitely wasn't Mr. Zauber in the barn, but maybe he knows something we don't."

"Like what?" Sophie laughed and hummed a scary tune. "It's haunted?"

I glared at her. "Exactly." I put my gloves back on and picked up my shovel. "You're laughing now, but you were running pretty fast earlier." I pushed the shovel hard into the ground and scooped up a clump of dirt.

"I told you. I didn't want to get in trouble. And see? We did. I was right."

I stopped digging and looked at her. "I wouldn't call that getting in trouble, but he's not acting like himself. Something's up."

Sophie nodded. "You're right about that. Something's up. As soon as we're done here, let's go back to the Coopers' and find out what." She picked up her shovel and started digging too.

We quit talking and worked nonstop for the next hour. My body ached like a job well done. Our little corner was a colorful dot on the greenway, bursting with the promise of the monarchs it would bring.

I pulled one of the magenta flowers from the bee balm bush to my nose and breathed in the sweet minty scent. A monarch landed on a flower and sucked up the nectar, as if she were drinking through a straw. Then she flew off and landed on milkweed. I really hoped she'd lay some eggs, and then more monarchs would come, then more, and slowly, one by one, we'd help save them from extinction.

※ ※ ※

When Mr. Zauber pulled back up in the UTV, his face looked long and serious. I hoped he wasn't still mad about us being at the Coopers'. "There's terrible news this morning, girls." He hopped out of the UTV, holding up his phone. "The *Black Mountain News* reports someone wants to build a ski resort on Paul's Peak."

"No!" Sophie yelled. Her face turned bright red.

Mr. Zauber wasn't making any sense. "What do you mean?" I asked. "A ski resort? In Black Mountain?"

"I can't believe it either," Mr. Zauber said. "Daryl Cooper must be rolling in his grave. He never wanted to sell."

A chill ran through me. Mr. Zauber was right. Daryl Cooper was rolling ... but not in his grave. It must've been his ghost we saw in the barn. Maybe that *is* why Mr. Zauber told us to stay away from the Coopers'. He must've seen it too.

"Then why are they selling it?" I asked. There were a bunch of headstones in that cemetery. Generations of Cooper ghosts could be unleashed.

Mr. Zauber shrugged. "He left it to his children. I guess they think they can do what they want with it. But ... that's not all." He paused and swallowed hard, like he couldn't get the words out. "They're going to ..." he paused again and cleared his throat, "umm ... petition the city to move and expand the road." His voice cracked. "And add a parking lot so there can be shuttle service from the resort to town." Sadness cascaded down his face as he looked across the garden toward Black Mountain Road.

"What? Where can they fit a parking lot?" I held my breath. No. Not here. Not the garden.

Mr. Zauber covered his face with his hands. "They want to take out part of the meadow and the butterfly garden," he said quietly.

"No!" I shouted, my stomach twisting in anger. "We have to stop them!"

Sophie jumped up, knocking over a stack of plastic flower containers. "There'll be no nectar for the monarchs!" Her voice shook. "No place for them to lay eggs!"

I pictured huge bulldozers crushing and ripping our flowers, leaving their petals chewed up and spit out all over the ground. A monarch sat on one of the coneflowers we'd just planted, opening and closing its majestic orange wings. They were already threatened. We couldn't let more of their habitat be destroyed. "We have to protest!" I yelled.

"You can protest at the zoning meeting Friday," Mr. Zauber said. "The zoning will have to be changed from residential to commercial before they can build it. Right now, the law says only houses can be built on that section of Black Mountain Road."

"We can make posters." I grabbed my backpack and slung it over my shoulders. "We'll hang them around town, and we can hold them up outside the courthouse."

"I can't protest since I'm a commissioner," Mr. Zuber said. "But I'll call your mom, Emma, and she and I will organize everyone from the Monarch Butterfly Project. You notify your environmental club."

"Let's start now!" Sophie yelled, running to her skateboard.

We said goodbye to Mr. Zauber and skated up the greenway trail and back out to the road. We made the quarter-mile to my house in record time.

Miss Bettie's truck was parked in the driveway. That meant Mom had already left to teach her morning biology class, and Miss Bettie was here to babysit my sister, Addie. We maneuvered around her old truck and left our boards on the porch. Kicking off our shoes by the door, we snuck in quietly so Addie wouldn't hear us. She was only eight and loved Sophie so much that she followed her around like a puppy. We didn't need the distraction today. We tiptoed up the stairs and past Addie's room to mine without saying a word. My brown and white spaniel, Cody, caught up to us and pushed his wet nose against my leg as he went into my room. I closed the door softly behind us.

I grabbed my tablet computer and plopped on my unmade bed. There was a text from Dad with a link to the newspaper article about the ski resort. Don't worry. Whoever's buying that land doesn't know who they're messing with. Mom and I are already on it. Can you make flyers to recruit people to sign a petition and to speak at the zoning meeting?

I sent Dad a thumbs-up. Then, I clicked on the Environmental Club group message and typed, Guys! Have you heard? Someone's trying to build a ski resort on Paul's Peak and THEY'RE TAKING OUT THE BUTTERFLY GARDEN!!!! Text back when you get this so we can meet up. We got work to do!!

Cody hopped on the bed and curled up next to me. He nosed my backpack, reminding me I still had some banana nut muffins Mom had made me for breakfast. I took one muffin out for me and handed the other to Sophie.

"Before we start the posters, let's think about how we can stop them," Sophie said as she paced back and forth across my flower rug, stuffing pieces of muffin into her mouth. "We could climb a tree and stay there. They couldn't chop them down if we were in them."

"Uh. Okay. Let's brainstorm and think of a bunch of stuff. That'll be number two." I wrote, Live in a tree in the notes app on my tablet. It was a dumb idea, but I knew not to stop Sophie now. She was fired up and needed to get it out of her system. "Number one is making posters and hanging them around town." I wrote as I talked.

Sophie went on like I'd never said a word. "Miss Bettie could bring us food. Addie will bring us water and books. We'll design a pulley system to bring it all up the tree." She stuffed the rest of the muffin into her mouth.

"I'll write that down, but let's think of something else. That's kind of drastic. Maybe that'd be a last resort if the other ideas wouldn't work."

"What other ideas? This *is* drastic!" Muffin crumbs flew out of her mouth as she yelled. "We're going to lose the monarchs! And what about the red wolves? There're less than twenty in the whole state of North Carolina. Where are they gonna go, Emma?"

"I know, Sophie. I care about the monarchs and the wolves too. We'll figure it out. Let's brainstorm first and think of details later. Like we did for the Earth Day walkout."

She plopped down on my bed and fell backward with her arms stretched out above her. She was breathing fast. Cody lay down next to her and licked the sticky muffin residue off her hands.

"Slow, deep breaths," I said. Sophie felt things deeply, all the way through to her bones. It was her best and worst quality. She threw her arm around Cody and closed her eyes as she breathed in and out slowly.

After a minute, her eyes popped open. "I've got an idea!" She hopped off the bed so quickly that Cody bounced in the air. "You know, if there's an endangered species living there, the Environmental Protection Agency probably won't let them build anything. It may be protected land!"

I nodded slowly, wincing about what she was going to say next.

"We've got to stake out and find the wolf. Do you think our parents will let us camp at the Peak?"

"No, I don't. We barely talked them into a sunrise hike." There was no way I'd ever camp near the haunted barn anyway. I'd never ask to do something that dumb.

"You're probably right. We'll have to look during the day."

I wrote, 3) Prove red wolves are on Paul's Peak.

Sophie was revved now but in a good way. She did a *grand jeté* to my desk and twirled around. "One more." She looked me in the eyes. "We need to speak at the zoning meeting."

Ugh. I'd rather face the haunted barn or live in a tree. "Umm, you remember what happened at our Earth Day Rally?"

She did. I could see it on her face.

In the middle of the rally, I'd felt like I had food in my teeth. That sent me into a panic that made me question everything. Was my zipper down? Was there peanut butter on my cheek? Did I have something gross on my nose? I completely lost my train of thought and stood there with my mouth open, staring at the crowd. Some of them laughed. Sophie jumped up and saved the day. She put her arm around me and started our Earth Day cheer to hype the crowd up and distract them. Thinking about it made fear prickles shoot through my body.

I shook my head. "They're not going to let us. We're kids."

"They might."

"I'll help you with the speech, but I'm not speaking." And I wasn't adding it to our list of things to do either.

"Mm-hmm." Sophie looked so sure of herself.

"Anyway," I said, "can you make the web page? I'm gonna get started on the posters."

Sophie knew me well enough to drop it, but I had a feeling this would not be the end of it. She slid into my desk chair and flipped open the laptop, her fingers flying over the keyboard. "No-blackmountainskiresort.com is open!" She beamed.

"Nice! I'll add it to the bottom of the posters."

Once we got the word out that the ski resort would destroy the butterfly garden and part of the meadow, the whole town would be against it. Everyone loved the butterfly garden. The town had a huge festival during migration season where volunteers caught and tagged butterflies in the meadow. There were usually hundreds of butterflies flying around and landing on bushes and flowers. Sophie and I liked to stand still with our arms out to see how many would land on us. Younger kids dressed up like pollinators and paraded down the greenway trail from the meadow to town. Tents lined the street, selling food and butterfly crafts.

I clicked open my drawing app and pulled up the poster I'd made to advertise the Monarch Festival last year. The picture of the meadow with the Peak in the background would work perfectly. I deleted all the festival stuff, and in the sky, I wrote, *Protect our Monarch Butterflies*. On the bottom corner, I added the info about the zoning meeting and wrote, *no-blackmountainskiresort.com*

Then, I mixed my yellow and red paints to create the bright bold oranges and golds of a monarch. I painted the butterfly in my sketchbook, took a picture, and opened it in the app. I wrote, *Save the Monarchs* in big black letters for our protest signs. It was perfect!

The monarch painting was also perfect for my summer art class journal. I looked up the definition of *intensity* and found: *how bright or dull a color is*. I wrote it above the butterfly.

The second definition of *intensity* was: *a strong feeling or sense of purpose*. Wasn't that the truth? I'd never felt this intense about anything. Sophie and I were worried and stressed out, but getting to work definitely helped our mood. I could tell Sophie felt better too. She hadn't said a word in over two hours. She hummed softly to herself.

I reformatted the two designs into flyers and then emailed everything to Dad and Sophie. I also texted one to the club group message. No one had responded to my other message yet. Those losers were probably still asleep.

"Done!" I rubbed Cody's velvety ears and kissed the brown spot on the top of his head. Then, I hopped up to check out Sophie's web page. She had links to different pages about monarchs and how bad deforestation was for the environment. "Ahh, you're amazing. That's *so* good."

"Look how well your meadow works for the banner," she said. "You're so talented."

"No, that's you. A total queen."

"We're a good team." She beamed as she scrolled down the page to show me a few more links. There was one to *The Truth About Red Wolves* page.

"Don't add the red wolf page yet," I said. "We have to prove they're there. I don't think anyone will believe us."

"No," she said. "I think we need to—"

"Just hold off for a bit. Focus on the monarchs."

She rolled her eyes. "Fine, but just for now. I *know* it's a red wolf." She shut the computer. "Let's skate to the diner to see if we can help my dad. Maybe we can overhear someone say who the buyers are."

"Great idea. I could go for a Black Mountain Cherry Cream Soda too."

I slid my tablet into my backpack, and we headed out.

Miss Bettie met us by the stairs. She usually had a warm smile, but today, she was scowling. "Y'all hear about the ski resort?" She shook the newspaper in front of us.

"Yeah. We're gonna fight it. Look at this." I pulled my tablet out and showed her the posters.

"Those are really good, Emma." Her eyes grew wide and serious. "You know, those buyers might be scared off if they learn about Black Mountain's history. Man-sized wolves lurking at the edge of the forest, kids vanishing in the middle of the day, ghosts of generations long past appearing in the shadows, odd music echoing through the mountains—"

"Those are stories people tell around the campfire," Sophie interrupted. "You don't actually believe them, do you?"

Miss Bettie shrugged. "People have been pretty convinced over the years. I'm saying if we spread those stories, maybe the ski resort won't like the bad publicity. Maybe they'll take it somewhere else. Just a thought."

"That's a great idea." I wrote, *4) Hype up the supernatural* to my list of ways to fight the ski resort. We had to go back to the Coopers' to find the red wolf and the ghost whether I wanted to or not. It might be the only way to save the Peak. A chill ran through me as I put my tablet back inside my backpack.

Chapter 3

Value: the lightness or darkness of colors

We always took the greenway to town. It was a little over a mile of twists and turns through the garden, meadow, and forest that made a perfect skateboard run. It wasn't crazy steep, just enough to get some speed with minimal effort. I put my arms out beside me and flitted through the warm air back and forth like the butterflies around me. The purple, blue, orange, and yellow flowers blurred by in a swirl of colors and sweet scents. I felt like I was flying inside one of Monet's paintings of his garden.

In the meadow, hundreds of milkweed plants dotted the grass like a rainbow exploded and left pieces of candy everywhere. I couldn't see the caterpillars, but they were there, munching their way through the milkweed as they prepared to become monarchs. All of them would be murdered by some heartless developer if our protest failed.

Sophie must've been thinking the same thing because she pushed off the ground with her right foot and flew ahead of me. I caught up to her, and we zoomed down the greenway.

We turned off onto Black Mountain Road. The shadows became longer as houses with big yards popped up between the trees, then houses with smaller yards, then townhouses with perfectly trimmed grass and flowers lining walkways, and then shops. The air smelled clean and fresh, as if the town had just hopped out of the shower and was ready for an exciting day.

We dodged a couple of people coming out of the coffee house, but I was thankful the sidewalk wasn't completely crowded yet. Later in the day, it'd be full of tourists sitting on rocking chairs, shopping in arts and craft stores, eating in restaurants, and listening to street performers playing bluegrass music.

The Walk light flashed at the crosswalk by Taco Heaven, so we kept going across the street without slowing down. We zoomed past the buildings, all of them pretty old, built when the train used to run in the 1800s. They had fancy brickwork around the rooflines and different colored awnings. It was like the town version of the garden. We sped by the purple awning on the art supply store, a blue one on the handmade jewelry store, a black music store, yellow honey store, pink cupcake bakery, and a burgundy antique shop. We zigged and zagged around a cell phone talker, a couple walking a dog, and a family with a stroller. We stopped our boards on the sidewalk in front of the diner.

Across the street, Dad was in our hardware store's big display window, picking up a wheelbarrow that had fallen over and spilled seed packets everywhere. The ghost of Eloise had struck again. Dad smiled and waved.

As I raised my arm to wave back, a huge black SUV with tinted windows stopped on the street in between us. It was so shiny that *Max's Diner* was reflected in the door like a mirror. I snapped a picture with my phone so I could draw it later for my summer art journal. Mrs. Hartford had told us to look for inspiration from the world around us, and the sign was perfect for the term *value*.

The door popped open, and out jumped two huge guys with short dark hair, wearing sunglasses and sport coats with khakis. One had on a maroon T-shirt, and the other wore a dark-gray one. Maroon-shirt-guy had a thin beard, and gray-shirt-guy had a goatee. Other than that, they looked exactly alike. Several people stopped and stared.

Gray-shirt-guy opened the door to the back seat, and out climbed a man in shiny black shoes and a very expensive navy suit—like the kind of suit I saw on YouTube during fashion week, not like the suit my dad got last year at the end-of-season sale at the mall. The guy had sunglasses, perfect skin, and longish brown hair.

A murmur went through the crowd. People seemed to recognize him.

We don't get many famous people in Black Mountain. Sometimes, they go to Asheville if they're making a movie nearby, but never here.

"Who's that?" I asked Sophie. "Are they filming something here?"

She shrugged.

Mrs. Patterson, the owner of Black Mountain Jewelry, moved in close to suit-guy, waving her phone. "Chester, can I have a picture?" Her voice was loud and squeaky, and her face was flushed. Maroon-shirt stepped in front of her, blocking her path.

"No, it's okay," suit-guy said. Flashing a very white smile, he leaned in next to Mrs. Patterson as she took a selfie.

This unleashed a herd of older women, waving their phones and descending on suit-guy, who I now figured out was Chester Scott, the middle-aged movie star known for a bunch of action movies he'd made about twenty years ago. He played a double agent, dodging bad guys and their bullets while he searched for ancient artifacts stolen during World War II. I wasn't sure what he'd done recently, but it didn't stop every mom and nana on the street from pushing in to get a glimpse of him.

A boy my age scooted across the seat and climbed out of the SUV, laughing as he watched the spectacle on the sidewalk. It couldn't be Jeb, but … whoa! It was! Wowza!

My stomach felt like I'd plunged down the Drop Tower ride at Carowinds. I grabbed Sophie's arm to steady myself. "Jeb Scott!" I whispered.

Well, I'd meant to whisper, but maybe I didn't because Jeb looked right at me and smiled. Perfectly straight white teeth and dimples. My face went hot. I looked away quickly but glanced back. He was still smiling at me.

Jeb was a lot cuter in person than on his Instagram. I would've thought it was the other way around. I'd been following him since he turned thirteen last summer and had a blowout birthday party where Petit Biscuit did a live show. He was taller than I'd imagined. Probably five foot seven. He had style too—ripped, faded jeans and a black T-shirt with a red-and-white checked pattern across the chest. I couldn't stop staring.

He followed Chester, who was snaking his way out of the crowd with help from maroon-shirt. When they got close, Jeb stared at my skateboard. "Wow. Cool deck." He looked at me and smiled again. "Where'd you get that board?"

My mind went blank. "Um … t-the mall … uhm … skate shop." My voice came out a hoarse croak like I'd swallowed a frog. Geez. Dork much?

He stopped right in front of me. "It looks kinda like that *Starry Night* painting my mom dragged me to go see at MoMA. Is that custom?" His voice was smooth and steady, like the shiny tall buildings in LA.

"Um … yeah, I-I guess. I painted it," I said, picking up my board. No croak but about three octaves higher than normal. Wait. He's seen van Gogh's *Starry Night*? I felt a little weak.

"Wow. Impressive. What's on the other side?"

I flipped it over and showed him the bottom of the deck where I'd painted more of the swirling blue sky and stars.

"I'd totally buy one. You do commissions?"

Gray-shirt stopped behind Jeb. "Come on, kid. Your dad's already in."

"See ya later, painter girl." Another smile.

My face burned as hot as the sunrise I'd watched in the morning. It was probably the same color too. The picture on my phone had come to life, talked to me, and walked into my best friend's restaurant. My head swirled in a dream fog. This couldn't be real.

Sophie and I looked at each other and then speed-walked to the door. Maroon-shirt blocked our way.

"Excuse me. We're getting lunch," I said, reaching around him for the door. His arm was bigger than my head.

"No one can go in right now," he practically growled as he stepped in front of me.

"This is my dad's diner." Sophie craned her next around maroon-shirt to see inside.

"Doesn't matter. No one can go in."

"Does my dad know about this?"

"Yes," maroon-shirt huffed as he stared over our heads. "Get lost, kids."

Sophie jumped up and down in front of the window, waving her arms to get Max's attention. He didn't see her. Or maybe he ignored her. I wasn't sure.

"Come on, Sophie." I dropped my board and hopped on. "Let's go."

"But—"

"We'll come back later." I tried to send her a message with my eyes. We could sneak in the back through the cellar window.

As I coasted toward the corner, she figured it out and hopped on her board. "Good idea," she said under her breath. That was the best part of our friendship. We didn't always need words.

We hid our boards in the alley, looked around to make sure no one was watching, and slid through the cellar window. I went first, right into a sticky, tangled cobweb.

"Gross! Watch out for the cobweb." I wiped my hands across my face and hair.

"I think you got it for me." Sophie giggled nervously.

The cellar felt damp and cold and smelled faintly of rotten fruit. We followed the beam of my phone's flashlight around boxes and crates to the wooden stairs and crept up slowly, crouching down.

"They're probably talking to your dad about filming a movie here," I whispered.

"Shhh," Sophie said.

"Do you think Jeb will be in it?"

"*Shhh*," Sophie said again, a little louder.

"Wait. Do you think we could be in … in a movie with *Jeb*?" I asked, completely forgetting to whisper. Stunned, I clamped my hand over my mouth.

Sophie put her finger to her lips and shot me her annoyed-mom glare. We stayed frozen in place on the stairs, waiting for someone to come, but luckily, no one did, so we kept climbing.

They must've been too busy talking about the movie to hear us. If they filmed in Max's Diner, Sophie and I could be extras. We could wait tables or sit behind Jeb and sip Black Mountain soda. Jeb didn't have anything on his Instagram about acting, so it must be something new. He mostly posted pictures of himself skateboarding and snowboarding.

We stopped when we reached the little hall behind the kitchen, and I held my breath and listened. The kitchen was quiet. The cook staff must've left, which was weird. Usually, four people cooked, and two waitresses helped Max during the lunch rush. He must've known Chester Scott was coming and sent everyone home.

I peeked around the corner and crawled across the cold black-and-white tiles like a ninja. Sophie followed. We made ourselves flat and scooted under the swinging door. Stopping behind the counter, we sat up quietly and stayed as still as possible.

Dishes clanked and forks scraped against plates. A voice drifted above us from a table near the counter. "Jeb's an excellent snowboarder," the guy, who must have been Chester, said. "I'm hoping he can run the resort when he's older."

All the air went out of my body like I'd been punched. Jeb and his dad were here to build the ski resort. It wasn't for a movie at all. This couldn't be happening. I'd finally gotten close to Jeb Scott, and he was destroying everything I loved. Tears shot to my eyes.

A deep baritone voice drifted above us next. It was the mayor, Frank Williams. I'd recognize his voice anywhere because he sounded like Mufasa from *The Lion King*. "I'll get the town on board," he said. "It'll be fantastic for our economy. There's a downturn here in the winter when the camps close and the hikers are gone. This will cause an economic boom."

Murmurs of agreement went around the table.

"I'll need your help, Max," the mayor said.

"You got it," Max said. "There'll be some pushback because of the environmental impact. Especially since we're gonna lose the butterfly garden and part of the meadow."

Sophie gasped. I couldn't imagine what it felt like to have your dad be a traitor. It was bad enough to realize my Instagram crush was behind this whole mess. My stomach still ached like I'd been punched.

"—and I'll get a petition going online and talk it up when folks come into the restaurant," Max continued.

Sophie deflated like a balloon that'd been held tight and let go. I put my arm around her to keep her from shooting off around the diner.

"Willa, what about your brother, Paul?" the mayor asked. "Will he interfere?"

"It's named after Paul, but Dad left it to me. The Peak is mine," Willa Cooper said. "My lawyer said there's nothing he can do."

"Why is it named after your brother?" Chester asked.

"He was in the scouts when he was a kid," Willa said. "For his project, he cleared a long trail that connected the public hiking trail to the peak. He wanted everyone to enjoy the view, even though it was on our property."

"How nice," Chester said. "We'll have to close off the public access though. No free rides."

"Of course. Paul hasn't lived in Black Mountain for years, so it really doesn't even concern him," Willa said.

"Good. Once we get this passed," Chester continued, "everyone will benefit. We'll include links to this restaurant and these other shops on our web page. I love Black Mountain. It hasn't changed a bit. Did you know I grew up nearby? Outside of Wilson."

Happy mummers of agreement drifted from the table. Of course, everyone knew that. He was the Swannanoa Valley's claim to fame, even though he moved away years ago.

"We used to drive over every Sunday afternoon when I was a kid," Chester said. "We ate here quite a bit, back when it was Stanley's. They had the best ice-cream sodas in Western North Carolina."

"Stanley was my uncle," Max said. The pride oozed out of his voice. "The citrus soda with vanilla ice cream was my favorite."

"My mom and dad loved that one too," Chester said. "They went to Stanley's on their first date. They both ordered the citrus and never looked back." He chuckled. "Jeb, we may owe our entire existence to Max's uncle's citrus ice-cream soda. Cool, huh?"

"Umm … sure." Jeb's voice moved toward us. "Can I grab a piece of pie?"

The pie was on the counter right above us. I held my breath. A stool at the counter creaked. A dish clanged.

A series of loud dings and vibrations shook my pocket. My phone! I jumped and hit my elbow hard against the counter as I fumbled with it, trying to shut it off. Some of the Environmental Club was finally responding. Wow, perfect timing, guys.

I looked up at the counter, expecting to find Max getting ready to yell at us, but instead, I saw Jeb staring right at me. Our eyes locked, and I froze.

"Everything okay, Jeb?" Chester asked.

"Yeah." He smiled at me while he pulled his phone up and pretended to check it, as if his had dinged, not mine. "I hit my knee on the counter. I'm good though."

The ache in my stomach turned into a butterfly and flitted around. Jeb smiled with his whole face, including the coolest hazel eyes I'd ever seen. They were almost the color of his hair but dark green around the iris with little green flecks sprinkled throughout. I took a mental picture so I could draw them later.

Sophie elbowed me. "Close your mouth," she whispered. "You look dumb."

I hadn't known it was open. "He's a lot cuter in person," I whispered.

Jeb laughed. "I can hear you," he whispered. "You guys better get out of here before Tweedledee and Tweedledum see you."

"This is my dad's restaurant. I can go where I want," Sophie said.

"Then why are you hiding behind the counter?"

"Tweedledum wouldn't let us in," I whispered.

Jeb laughed again. "Actually, that was Tweedledee."

"Jeb, who are you talking to?" Chester asked.

Sophie and I froze.

"No one. I'm working on some lyrics and said them out loud. Can I have a pen and some paper?"

"Sure," Max said. "There's some behind the counter." A chair scooted and the floorboards creaked. Max must have stood to come behind the counter. Sophie and I looked at each other, eyes wide. How much trouble could we get into? He never told us to keep out.

"That's all right. I'll get it." Jeb came flying over the counter and landed a few feet from us. "I've always wanted to do that." He laughed. "Just tell me where."

"Under the register."

Jeb walked by us, grabbed a piece of paper and pen and jumped back over.

The group at the table went back to their conversation about the ski resort. Willa and Max made a plan to get support together for the zoning meeting. Things were about to get ugly. Everyone loved the Peak and the garden, so the whole town would fight this group. Nobody would let them destroy it.

A paper airplane flew over the counter and hit me on the head. It was a note from Jeb with his phone number! **I'm bored. Where's a good place to skate? Text me if you want to hang.**

Wowza! Wowza!

I felt like I was going to throw up. Jeb Scott gave us his number! My mind went numb. Sophie read the note over my shoulder and rolled her eyes.

"Once the zoning gets approved, we'll finalize the numbers," Chester said. Several chairs scraped across the floor at the same time.

Sophie shook my shoulder and pointed to the swinging door. I crawled out behind her, stopping to give Jeb a thumbs-up, so he'd know I'd text him as soon as it was safe.

We snuck down the stairs and climbed out through the window to the alley, stopping to brush the dirt off our knees before we pulled our skateboards out of their hiding spots.

"Let's get some lunch and interrogate my dad," Sophie said as she hopped on her board. "I can't believe he's for this."

We rode around to the front of the diner right as Chester Scott and his entourage came out. Jeb walked by us and winked. My stomach did that weird flip-flop thing again.

"Quit staring," Sophie said, pulling my arm. "Let's find my dad."

When we stormed into the diner, Max looked up from clearing the table and smiled. "I'm glad you're here. You all can help."

Sophie put her hands on her hips. "Where's everyone else?"

"I sent everyone home until we reopen for dinner. Here, take these to the kitchen." He pushed a stack of plates toward her, but she didn't move.

"Why did you send them home?" Sophie's eyes were dark and angry.

I zoned out of the conversation and stared at my phone and Jeb's note, trying to get up the courage to text him. What would I even say?

"Emma, can you get the flatware?" Max set a gray dishpan on the table in front of me, and I stuck the note and my phone in my backpack.

Sophie kept glaring at Max. "Don't help him until he tells us what's going on."

I picked up the dishpan and hovered above the table, unsure if I should listen to Max or Sophie. I would never talk to my dad like Sophie did. I'd definitely get grounded for life, but that wasn't the only reason. It seemed so … I don't know, rude. But, then again, Max didn't always treat Sophie the best either. Ever since her parents had gotten divorced, she and Max seemed to go round and round, stuck in a circle of disrespect.

"I had important customers," Max said. "They rented the whole restaurant. Now stop being pigheaded and take these to the kitchen." He pushed the plates toward Sophie again.

I picked up the flatware and dropped them into the dishpan. Sophie shook her head, but I didn't stop. "We saw Chester Scott, Dad. Everyone saw him. He's the one buying the Cooper property, isn't he?"

Max sighed. "It was a confidential meeting. I don't discuss what my patrons say in my restaurant."

"I can't believe you're for the ski resort." She picked up the dishes, carried them to the counter, and set them down hard. They rattled and clanged. "I'm calling Mom."

"She's still on the plane. She doesn't land until about midnight, our time." Max scrubbed a spot on the table.

"I'll call her then."

"There's nothing she can do, Sophie. I'm not the only one supporting the ski resort. The wheels are in motion."

Suddenly, the diner door flew open and my dad came stomping through. "So, that's why you closed for lunch?" He glared at Max. "You knew about this, didn't you?"

"It'll be great for business, Jimmy." Max went behind the counter and put Dad's to-go order in a brown bag. "A five-star resort with big spenders. You could expand your store. Buy that building next door. And my barbecue would reach a bigger market—Max's World-Famous Barbeque." He handed Dad his order and then stared dreamily out the restaurant window. I could practically see dollar signs in his eyes.

"A few extra bucks in our pocket isn't worth the damage. It'll change the whole ecological landscape of Black Mountain." Dad's face was red. "A ski resort will bring in way too many people. There'll be more trash, more traffic, more pollution. We have to stop it!"

"And what about the monarchs that roost here on their way to Mexico?" Sophie said.

"And all the animals on Paul's Peak." I glanced at Sophie. Like the red wolf. What if it's a mama wolf with babies?

"It's only a few acres." Max said. "There's lots of places for the monarchs and animals to go, girls."

Dad scowled. "Don't be patronizing, Max. Our girls understand the environmental impacts more than both of us. It's their thing." He handed Max the cash for his lunch. "I'm going to the zoning meeting to fight this."

"So are we," Sophie said, looping her arm through mine. "I want pizza for lunch. Let's go to Antonia's, Emma."

"You're against it now," Max said as we headed to the door, "but you won't be when all of the money rolls in. We could take that trip to Sweden you've been dreaming about, Sophie."

Ugh. I was definitely going to draw Max's sign for my summer art journal. I'd write two meanings of the word *value—the lightness or darkness of a color* and *how much something is worth*. Max thought his business was worth more than the monarchs, more than the garden, and more than Paul's Peak. His values were all wrong.

We followed Dad out the door, and Sophie slammed it shut behind us. "I can't believe all this is happening the week Mom is gone, and I'm stuck at his house. He doesn't care about me at all."

"It's not personal, Sophie," my dad said. "He's always wanted to grow his restaurant, and he can't see past that right now. Keep talking to him. I think he'll come around."

The three of us stopped and looked up at the Peak, which sat to our right, behind the park. The trees looked like thick green fur—like I could jump down from the periwinkle sky and hug their soft fluffy leaves. With ski runs instead of trees, it would look like one of those hairless cats people with allergies get. Some things should be left alone. Cats need hair, and mountains need trees.

Dad turned from the mountain and smiled at us. "Awesome work this morning, girls. We make a great team. I've already gotten fifteen signatures on the petition, and it's been out less than an hour. Don't worry. We got this."

If Dad were a color, he'd be a calming teal like the late afternoon ocean. His confidence splashed off him and sprayed onto everyone around him. He gave us each a fist-bump, and then he crossed the street and disappeared into our store. The bell on the door jingled as it swung closed.

Antonia met us at the front of her restaurant with a huge smile. "Everybody's talking, talking, talking about Chester Scott. Did you see him? I missed the whole thing." She gestured out the window toward Max's Diner.

"We saw him." Sophie pushed the words out hard, like they hurt. "He's the one buying the Cooper property."

Her smile melted into a frown. "Well, what'd you know? Chester Scott is the mystery buyer. That will be hard to stop." She led us through the crowded restaurant to the last empty booth. The whole place was swamped with tourists and locals chatting nosily. Most were talking, not eating.

Last year, Antonia had taught me and Sophie how to pronounce the Italian words on the menu correctly, which we usually did loudly to impress the tourists. Today, we just ordered a cheese pizza, breadsticks, and two Black Mountain Cherry Cream Sodas.

Neither one of us ate much. Sophie wanted to talk about the conversation we'd overheard at Max's, but my mind kept drifting back to Jeb. I really wanted to text him, but my brain couldn't stir up words. I kept replaying images—his smile, the note flying over the counter and hitting me on the head, his wink as he walked out of the restaurant ... I shook my head to clear it and opened the note section of my phone to practice. Hello, I typed. I quickly backspaced over it and typed, Hey.

"You don't need to respond to the group message. I already did," Sophie said. "Evelyn and Cami are meeting us tomorrow to pass out the posters and flyers. Brie's at the beach, and Jayden's at his grandma's in Mississippi. I don't know about anyone else."

"What? Oh ... I'm not. I'm thinking about what I'm gonna text Jeb."

Sophie's face went from confused to shocked to angry in about three seconds. "You're not actually texting him, are you? He's a gross, spoiled, rich kid!" She was almost yelling. A few heads snapped toward our table.

"Shh. You're being too loud. And you don't even know him," I said quietly.

She glanced around at the people staring and lowered her voice. "You heard his dad. He's destroying the whole mountain so Jeb has a place to snowboard. This is all his fault."

"What's that saying?" I asked. "'Keep your friends close but your enemies closer?' We should find out everything we can about the buyer."

She let out an exasperated sigh. "I know everything I need to know."

Ugh. Sophie would never hang out with Jeb. She hated him, and she hadn't even met him yet.

I needed privacy. I couldn't text with her huffing and puffing across from me. "I'm going to the bathroom. Can you ask Antonia to refill my cream soda?"

I slid out of the booth and weaved around the tables and chairs to the bathroom by the kitchen. I went into a stall and closed the door. Hey Jeb. It's Emma from Max's restaurant. I typed into my notes, heart racing. Meet us at the trail on the greenway at 1:30. We'll be at trail marker 3. I added a smiley face but erased it. I copied the note to messages, typed in his number, held my breath, and sent it.

Once he saw the garden and the meadow, he'd change his mind about tearing it down. He had to.

Chapter 4

Perspective: creating an illusion of height, width, depth, and distance on a flat surface

After lunch, Sophie and I skated to the greenway to finish pulling weeds in the butterfly garden. We stopped on the trail and took it all in—singing birds, whooshing trees, sunlight changing the color of the flowers as it danced across them. We could see the whole spectrum, each color from its brightest to deepest hue. It was a paradise. Why would anyone want to bulldoze it into the ground and cover it with blacktop? What kind of person would even think to do that?

A monarch flitted past us and landed on the orange butterfly weed. Sophie sucked in her breath. "Do you think it'll lay eggs?" she whispered, as if her voice would scare it away.

"I hope so." I pulled out my phone and made a video of the butterfly as it flew over to the coneflower.

My phone buzzed. It was Jeb! My legs wobbled and sent me down into the soft grass as I opened his text message.

Told Dad I want to skateboard on the greenway trail. He's cool with it. TBH, I thought he'd snuff that idea. He wants to send me with Tweedledum. Trying to talk him out of it. Give me a sec.

"Jeb's coming," I said, trying to play it cool, but my voice cracked. "Maybe with the bodyguard though."

Sophie glared at me. "I knew you went into the bathroom to text him. You only wanna hang with him because he's famous." She dropped her backpack and started yanking weeds and slamming them on the grass.

"Not true. I'm gonna show him the garden to change his mind about building the resort. Once we change his mind, he can convince his dad." I flipped my camera to selfie mode and checked my hair. It was a stringy mess, but there was no time to braid. I slid my hair tie off my wrist and redid my ponytail. "Besides, he seemed really nice. It'll be fun."

"You barely talked to him." Sophie pulled on a dandelion, but the root wouldn't come.

I put on lip balm, checked myself out in my phone one more time, and gave up. I scooted over next to her. "Let me see if I can loosen the roots," I said, picking up a stick. "We need to bring a shovel next time."

She scooted away from me to work on a different section. "We need to get started on our list of ways to stop the resort, not waste our time with a gross, spoiled, rich kid."

I stopped wiggling the stick and turned toward her. "I'm not wasting time. Like I said, we have to convince him not to build it. I'm adding *change the enemy's mind* to our list."

Sophie grunted. "Fat chance."

Something rolled on the trail behind me. I spun around. It was Jeb riding his skateboard. He turned the corner and jumped up, kicking the board with his back foot so it flipped around sideways in a three-sixty.

My stomach did a three-sixty too, like I was the board being kickflipped.

He guided the board back to the ground and kept on skating, stopping on the pavement in front of us. He hopped off and flipped it up with his foot, catching it in his hand. It had a really cool graphic painted in black, white, and red on the deck.

"Hey," he said.

"Hey," I said back, but my voice came out two octaves higher than normal. I hopped up quickly, wobbled, and almost fell. What was wrong with me? "Nice board."

"Thanks. It's a Jesse Marxx original. Yours is nice too. I'm serious about that commission. You wanna draw something up and text it to me?"

I nodded.

"Great. So, you guys should know I have a girlfriend," Jeb said.

"Good for you." Sophie rolled her eyes and turned back to the weeds.

"I didn't want you to get the wrong idea when I tossed you my number. I'm just looking for people to skate with."

I wasn't going to admit it, but I was disappointed. "Thanks for letting us know," I squeaked. Why couldn't I control my voice? "We just wanna skate too."

"*Emma* wants to skate with you." Sophie slammed some clover into her pile of weeds. "*I* don't."

"That was stupid. Forget I said that," Jeb said. "Let's start over. I'm Jeb." He moved his board to his left hand and stuck out his right for Sophie to shake.

"Geez, boomer. We're shaking hands now?" She stayed on the ground and didn't reach for his hand.

I stepped in front of her and took his hand. "Nice to meet you, Jeb. I'm Emma, and this is Sophie." When we let go, the dirt from my hand was all over his. He didn't seem to care, but I felt redness creeping from my neck to my face as he wiped it off on his jeans.

"Why does Sophie hate me?" Jeb asked.

"She doesn't hate you. She's mad about the ski resort." I still couldn't get my voice to sound normal.

"Why? It's gonna be amazing." He spent the next several minutes describing the runs they were going to build for snowboarding. He told us about the steepness of the hills and how fast they'd be. He explained how the snow machines will work if it didn't snow enough. He went on and on and on.

The more he talked, the angrier Sophie became. She kept pulling the weeds harder and harder, accidentally pulling a piece of milkweed. "Crap," she said, laying the milkweed back down in the garden. "You think it'll germinate if I leave it?"

"What?" Jeb finally stopped talking about the resort.

"She pulled a flower instead of a weed," I said. Jeb looked confused. I turned toward Sophie. "I think so. Let's bag up these weeds. That's enough. Don't you think?"

"Do you guys snowboard?" Jeb asked.

"We do, but there's lots of places to go. We don't need to snowboard here." Sophie picked up the bag she'd left earlier and shoved the weeds into it. If she wasn't careful, she was going to rip it. "You're gonna destroy our garden and our mountain."

Jeb dropped his board and picked up some of the weeds. He placed them gently in the bag. "These flowers are gonna die in the winter anyway, right? You can plant the new ones somewhere else."

Sophie's mouth flew open, and her face turned bright red. She tried to speak but she was so mad she couldn't get the words out.

"No," I said. "These are perennials. They come back every year." My voice finally sounded normal. I needed to focus on saving the garden and the mountain, not on how cute Jeb was. "See that bush with the pink flowers?" I pointed to the huge bee balm on the other side of the garden. "That's where they started planting the monarch garden fifteen years ago. That bush is older than us, and you want to rip it up."

Jeb shrugged.

"And we just planted all these." Sophie waved to our part of the garden. "We spent all morning planting these flowers that will grow for years and years and give food to thousands of pollinators."

"And as for the mountain," I added, "monarchs roost in the trees there every fall, and lots of animals live there. Where are they supposed to go?"

Jeb shrugged. "I never thought about it."

"Well, you should." Sophie pointed at him angrily. "Red wolves are going extinct because of people like you. There's less than twenty left in the world, and they're all here in North Carolina. Emma and I heard one on the Coopers' property." Her voice got louder and louder as she continued. "If you build your stupid ski resort, they'll have no place to go. The wolves will die!"

I could tell by the look on Jeb's face that he regretted meeting us. He just wanted to skate. He didn't sign up for our lecture entitled *The Environmental Impact of Jeb Scott's Terrible Choices*. We needed a different tactic. Screaming at him wasn't going to change his mind.

And now there was no way Sophie would ever like him. She took it personally when people didn't care about animals. Last fall, when a group of hunters had stopped at Max's for breakfast, she served them decaf coffee instead of regular and put salt in their sugar bowl. She'd wanted to stick a nail in their tire so they'd be stuck, but I talked her out of that.

But if I could get Jeb to care about the environment, it'd be two wins. Sophie would like him, and he and his dad wouldn't build the ski resort. I had the perfect plan. "Have you been on the property yet?" I asked.

"No. Dad showed me pictures. He's gonna take me there once it's actually for sale."

"Let's show him," I said, turning back to Sophie. "We'll skate down the greenway and hike to Paul's Peak. We'll point out all the things we love and how it will change if they build on it."

"It won't make a difference," Sophie said.

"Probably not." Jeb grabbed his board with his foot and spun it around. "But let's do it. I wanna see it."

"You might wanna change your shoes," I said, eyeing his bougie white high-tops. "It'll be muddy."

"Naw. It's all good. These are my old ones." He hopped on his board and tick-tacked in circles around us. "Coolio. Lead the way, ladies!"

Sophie rolled her eyes. "'Coolio,'" she repeated mockingly. "Seriously?"

Jeb shrugged. "We going or not?"

Sophie and I got on our boards and headed up the greenway trail. Jeb skated next to me, and as we rode, I explained to him how monarch butterflies migrated through Black Mountain every year around October, and I pointed out the plants that gave them energy.

We glided around the corner and out popped Cami Suárez, secretary of our environmental club, being pulled by Poncho the overly peppy poodle. Jeb swerved to the left, barely missing them.

"Vaya! Watch where you're going, bruh." Cami pulled Poncho into the grass, but the huge black dog immediately ran back and jumped on Jeb, knocking him off his board.

"You watch out," Jeb said as he tried to wiggle out from under Poncho's paws. The dog was almost as tall as Jeb.

Cami laughed. "I should warn you. He's a licker."

"Get him off me."

Sophie and I helped Cami pull Poncho off. Then Cami bribed him with treats to get him back to the grass. If Cami were a color, she'd be bright orange—a little chaotic but full of fun.

"You just move here or something?" Cami asked as she wound the leash around her hand and gripped it tighter.

"This is the guy who's going to bulldoze the greenway and tear up the Peak so he can ski," Sophie said.

Jeb's face turned red.

"Oh, yeah. You're that Jeb Scott kid. I think I follow you on Instagram. I'm Cami, pet-sitter extraordinária." She handed him her card. Cami was all about business. She was already saving so she could go to vet school.

Jeb took the card and examined it. "What's an extraordinária?"

"You know, like, extraordinary, astounding, the best, most knowledgeable pet-sitter in Black Mountain."

"Nice." Jeb stuck the card in his pocket.

"Do you have a pet?"

"A cat, but he's in LA."

"Okay, I'm gonna need that card back then. Let me know if you get a dog." She held out her hand, and Jeb gave the card back to her.

"So, you're more like a dog walker or something?"

"No. Well, mostly dogs. I tried to walk Mrs. Patterson's cat once. It didn't go well. But I don't only walk. I feed, bathe, play with—but now that I'm thinking about it, it's mostly dogs. Cats don't need a sitter. Right, Poncho?"

The dog thumped his tail against the grass.

"So, you're more like a dog-sitter extraordinária." Jeb scratched Poncho behind his ears.

"Sure, but—"

"Cami," I said. "We were explaining to Jeb about the monarchs and why we need to save the garden and Peak. Maybe you can tell him about the migration to Mexico."

"Monarchs are the orange and black ones, right?" Jeb asked. "Like that one?" He stopped petting Poncho and pointed to a butterfly that had landed on some butterfly weed. Its bright wings opened and closed while it sucked out the nectar from the orange flower.

"Yeah, that's one," I said. "It takes four generations to make it across the US from Mexico and then back. So that one could be the great-grandkid of the ones that came through last year."

"How do they know where to go, then?"

"That's the amazing part," I said. "Nobody knows. It could be they follow the sun, or maybe they have a magnetic compass. I think it's in their DNA. Somehow, the generations are passing down the memories through their DNA."

The butterfly flew off the bush and flitted away.

"They only eat and lay their eggs on milkweed," Cami said. "That's why we've planted a bunch on the greenway and in the meadow. My dad's an expert. He grew up in Michoacán, Mexico, where the Butterfly Reserve is. He works with Mexico's Commission for Natural Protected Areas, and he also teaches at the University of Asheville with Emma's mom. Every winter break, he takes students to the reserve, so he *knows* what he's talking about. He said there was way less last year because there's not as much milkweed or places for them to roost. You can't go bulldozing milkweed, bruh. Even a little. They need it."

Poncho let out a huge "woof" and lunged after a squirrel, pulling Cami with him.

"Stay, Poncho! Stay!" she yelled, but he kept going. "Okay. Bye, guys! See you tomorrow. Hasta luego, bulldozer dude!" she yelled over her shoulder.

"It's Jeb!" he yelled back, looking annoyed as he jumped on his board and pushed off the pavement.

I skated next to him.

"I thought they were just bugs," he said. "I didn't know they were so complicated."

"They're very complicated. Cami's not exaggerating. Without milkweed, they'd go extinct."

"It's already happening," Sophie said as she caught up to us. "It's even worse than Cami said. There're eighty percent fewer monarchs now than thirty years ago. And, for the western monarchs—the ones in your part of the country—there used to be over four million that migrated. Now there's only thirty thousand. You want to know why?"

"Let me guess." Jeb sighed. "What is commercial development?"

"You win. But this isn't a game show. Monarchs are pollinators. Everyone loses, but especially the monarchs."

"Don't you think about anything besides the environment?" Jeb stopped his board and scowled at her.

"Don't you think about anything besides yourself?" Sophie snapped.

Ugh. I actually had him interested in butterfly migration for a couple of minutes. We were never going to change his mind if Sophie didn't lighten up.

We skated in silence. When we got to my yard, I stopped and kicked my board to the grass. "Let's leave our boards here and walk the rest of the way."

Jeb hugged his board to his chest. "You drop your stuff in your front yard, and no one steals it?"

"Yeah, it's fine. But if you want, you can stick it under the porch. Be quiet though. If my little sister sees us, she'll wanna come."

Sophie and I waited for him while he hid his board. Then, the three of us crossed the street and walked in the grass along the side of the road. We kept going until we reached the fence that divided the Zaubers' property from the Coopers'.

When we stopped in the tree's shadows, my heart raced with the memory of bursting out of the woods and running for my life. I'd been so focused on showing Jeb the beauty of the mountain, I completely forgot about the danger. "Let's walk by the fence line. It'll be harder because there's no trail, but this way, we stay away from the barn."

A cool breeze rustled the leaves. They sounded like whispers, telling us to turn back. A little shiver ran down my spine.

"Why are we staying away from the barn?" Jeb asked.

The breeze blew my hair in my eyes. I pushed the stray hairs behind my ear and side-eyed Jeb. "It's haunted."

Jeb went white. "Haunted?"

"There's a family graveyard on the property. Didn't your dad tell you?"

"No," he said, his hazel eyes wide. "But, so what? I don't believe in that stupid supernatural crap. No one does."

He talked a good game, but he was clearly spooked. Maybe instead of trying to get him interested in the environment, we could try number five on my list: scare him out of buying the property. It wouldn't be hard. I was spooked too.

"Yeah, you'll have to leave the bodies there when you build. You can't move *dead* bodies," Sophie said.

"Daryl Cooper and his ancestors have returned," I said. "To haunt you all. That land's been in his family for generations. He never wanted to sell."

Ugh. Generations of Cooper ghosts could be unleashed. I did a quick scan around us. This was why I never told ghost stories. I always scared myself.

"You guys are full of it." Jeb squinted through the trees. "You're just messing with me."

"No, it's true," I said. "Sophie and I saw something moving in the barn window."

"Maybe somebody's camping out. A hiker or something." Jeb sounded like he was trying to convince himself, not us. His face was still white, and he kept looking over his shoulder.

"You need to research Black Mountain before you build your ski resort here. It's a spiritual vortex. All kinds of strange stuff happens," Sophie said. "Like years ago, some kids drowned in the Swannanoa River." She pointed to the fence surrounding Mr. Zauber's farm. "Right over there. Ever since then, River Girl has haunted the river from the Zaubers' all the way to Camp Eagle Crest."

"The whole town's haunted," I added as the tingle in my spine moved to my arms and then down to my fingertips.

Jeb took a couple of paces back and forth in the grass. He acted like he wanted to run away, never seeing us again. "I thought you brought me out here to show me how pretty it is. Not scare me."

"Facts are facts," Sophie said. "We want you to be aware." She pushed open a leafy bush and peeked around it.

"If you're too scared, we don't have to go." I tried to keep my voice steady, but it cracked.

"I'm not scared," he said, his eyes meeting mine.

Dang, he had beautiful eyes. I felt a little guilty for trying to scare him. "All right, then, let's do this." I forced a smile, hopefully in a reassuring way.

Sophie picked her way through the underbrush, and Jeb and I followed. Usually, my mind wandered in the woods, but I stayed alert, listening for the ghost as we pushed our way through the thick weeds, vines, and saplings. The birds that had serenaded us this morning were replaced by the loud chirping and buzzing of the cicadas. They made it hard to hear anything else.

But when we made it to the trail, something cracked and popped so loud, nothing could drown it out.

I jumped, tingling all over.

Jeb stopped. "What was that?"

"Probably a ghost." Sophie crouched down with her phone out, scanning the woods. I'm pretty sure she was looking for the red wolf, not a ghost.

"Ha ha," Jeb said, but he wasn't laughing.

I peered through the waving leaves. A squirrel scurried across a dead oak that lay across the mossy ground. I let out a shaky breath. "Just a squirrel." I took a few deep breaths to get rid of the creepy feeling and to focus on the beauty around me.

We followed the trail to the top where it stopped and circled two large rocks. We took the circle counterclockwise to its dramatic reveal—a gap in the trees where the whole world opened. Up here, I always felt like an eagle perched high on a tree. I could see for miles.

In the distance, mountains looped and crossed each other in hazy waves of blue. Cottony clouds swished through the sky that wasn't only blue but glowing in shades ranging from royal to turquoise to white. Around us, trees grew up the mountains, splashing hues of greens.

Jeb gasped. "Whoa! Can't you see it with snow everywhere? Look at that vertical drop! I'll race down the slope and do a three-sixty on a jump we'll put in over there. Then, I'll fly back up on the ski lift higher than that bird." He turned to face us. "You guys are gonna love it."

Sophie looked at me, panicked. This wasn't working out the way I'd hoped. "That bird," she snapped, "is a bald eagle. They were going extinct a few years ago, but they brought some here to North Carolina. Now there're hundreds. Once you tear down the trees, where will they nest?"

"Look around. There're thousands of trees on the other mountains."

"You don't get it." Sophie turned and walked away.

"You can do all of that stuff at Cataloochee or Wolf Creek Ski Resort." I tried to sound reasonable and not yell, but my stomach felt like it was full of huge rocks that twisted all the way up into my throat. "Or any of the other bazillion ski resorts nearby. We don't need another resort here. Buy one of those." I took a deep breath and blew it out, trying to unravel my stomach.

"Dad's pretty set on Black Mountain. Reminds him of being a kid or something."

I opened my mouth, but my emotions were so tangled, nothing came out. I plopped down, settling into the cool shade of my favorite oak and got out my sketchbook. Drawing always relaxed me.

Jeb stared at me. "What are you doing?"

"We're gonna show you why we love it up here. Why it's wrong to destroy it."

Sophie wiped her eyes with the back of her hand and sat down too.

"Sit still and listen." I dug through my backpack to find my pencil.

"What am I listening to?" Jeb asked as he sat down. "I can only hear that annoying buzzing—*doopdoop doopdoop pshewpshew chrill chrill chrill*. What the heck is that?"

I laughed, the knots in my stomach loosening a little. "Cicadas. You do a pretty good impression."

"They're crazy loud."

"When there's a bunch together in an area, they synchronize their songs. They're trying to attract females," Sophie said.

"Good luck to them." Jeb laughed.

"Ignore them," I said. "If you're lucky, you might hear the red wolf howl. If you're really still, a deer or rabbit might come by."

"You just sit here?" He already sounded bored.

"I draw, and Sophie writes. Don't you write songs?" I pulled a notebook and pen out of my backpack and held them out to him.

"Like the cicadas," Sophie said.

"What?" The annoyance in Jeb's voice bounced off his question like he knew what she was going to say next.

"Creating songs to attract females." Sophie laughed as she leaned back against a tree and pulled out her notebook.

Jeb rolled his eyes. "I have an app," he said, but he took the notebook from me.

"You can't talk." Sophie put her notebook on her lap. "Not for at least thirty minutes. Longer if somebody gets in the zone."

"Zone?"

"When everything's flowing, like it's not even you doing it. Like time's stopped, and you're somewhere else," Sophie said.

Jeb nodded slowly. "Once, when I was mixing and playing music, I accidentally stayed up all night long."

"So, you get it." Sophie almost smiled. Maybe she was warming up to him. This could be good. "Thirty minutes start ... now." She set the timer on her phone.

Jeb set the notebook next to him and lay back with his hands behind his head. Sighing loudly, he closed his eyes and wiggled around to get comfortable.

I flipped my sketchbook to a blank page and drew his profile. He had really nice angles. I sketched from under his ear to his cheekbone and followed the line to his chin. It was square with a little indention. Then, I drew the line from his chin to his lips, over his nose, down the little slope, and up to his forehead. I filled in his eyebrows and eyes—deep set with visible lashes—then added the side of his nose and lips. His hair was easy to draw. It swooshed over his forehead and was tighter at the sides. I wished I had my pastels so I could capture the color. It was brown, but it had an auburn tint.

Some guys were cute, but Jeb passed that. He was next level. Maybe a ski resort wouldn't be the end of the world. Jeb would be across the street from me every winter. We could snowboard together. I looked out over the mountain, imagining it treeless and covered in white fluffy snow. I'd fly down the mountain in front of him, but I'd wipe out. He'd stop and help me up like in one of those romantic Christmas movies Mom loves to watch. He'd slip too, so we'd fall into the snow together. Then ... *NO* ... what was *wrong* with me? I set my pencil down and put my face in my hands. How could I sell out the wolves, eagles, and butterflies for a hazel-eyed guy with a great smile?

When I looked up, Sophie was staring at me. She looked at my sketch pad and then back up at me with wide eyes that asked, *What are you doing?*

I shrugged and shook my head. I didn't actually know what I was doing. Something had possessed me. I avoided her glare by looking down and turning to a clean page. I forced all thoughts of Jeb out of my head and concentrated on drawing. I sketched butterflies flying around with nowhere to land and a red wolf standing below, looking sadly around the treeless mountain. I'd show it to Mrs. Hartford for the term *perspective*, then I'd hang it in my room to keep me focused. I needed to keep my perspective. Jeb was cute and seemed nice, but the butterfly garden and Paul's Peak were more important. I had to remember that.

Chapter 5

Form: a three-dimensional shape that shows length, width, and depth

The swishing leaves must have made Jeb sleepy. He jumped when his phone chimed, and yawned and stretched before checking the message. "That was Tweedledum. He's waiting for me at the bottom of the greenway trail," he said, hopping up. He brushed the dirt from his jeans and let out a little scream. "What's that?" He knocked a bright green bug off his pant leg.

"It's a praying mantis," I said.

"Does it bite?"

"Seriously?" Sophie laughed. "Yes. See its huge fangs?"

"Fangs!" Jeb yelled, eyes wide. He did a hopping dance to get out of its way.

"You're not a grasshopper, Jeb," I said as I stood. "It doesn't want to eat you."

"Geez. It's terrifying." He searched around his T-shirt as he brushed the leaves off. When he was satisfied there were no more bugs, he snapped a picture of the view from the Peak. "I'm sending this to my cousin. He's gonna flip."

I snapped a picture too and stood for a minute while the treetops danced and waved in the wind. I wanted to promise them I'd do everything I could to keep them from being ripped up and shredded. I wanted to tell them everything would be okay, but I didn't. That would've been weird.

Sophie led the way down the trail. We followed it for a bit and then veered off to avoid the barn. We weaved around the trees, avoiding the sticker bushes in the underbrush. Shadows bounced through the trees like ghosts. At least, I think they were shadows.

A low, deep howl came from the trees ahead of us.

We froze.

"What was that?" Jeb whispered.

"That's the red wolf!" Sophie pulled out her phone. "I need to get a video."

"How do you know it's a wolf?" Jeb asked.

"We looked it up," I said as I pulled my phone out of my backpack. "Wolves' howls are low and deep. Like that."

"And they sound sad. I think it's because there aren't many left. They're lonely." Sophie sounded sad too.

Jeb looked nervously through the trees. "Are they dangerous?"

"Only if you're a raccoon or something," I said. "They've never attacked a person. Ever."

"Well … they *could* though," Sophie said. She was just trying to scare Jeb.

"No, they wouldn't," I said. "The biggest animal they'll take down is a deer. And it's usually a sick one."

Sophie bent down and pushed a leaf over. Underneath, there was a huge paw print in the mud. HUGE!

"What the heck? That's *really* big," I said, kneeling next to Sophie. "That can't be a red wolf." I compared the print to the size of my hand. It was way bigger. That couldn't be right. Sophie and I both took pictures.

Jeb bent down a few feet in front of us. "Here's another one! Geez, is that its stride?"

I walked over to Jeb and took a picture of the print. "It can't be. That's too long. Some of the prints must not have stuck."

Sophie ran ahead. "Here's another!"

We followed more paw prints down the mountain next to the Zaubers' fence, but then they stopped. We searched all around but didn't see any more.

"It couldn't have jumped the fence, could it?" A chill went through me. Something wasn't adding up. What kind of wolf left huge prints and had long strides?

Sophie's eyebrows were scrunched up. "I don't think so ... but maybe?"

I walked up to the fence. It had to be at least eight feet high. On the other side, about three feet from the last paw print, there was a human footprint. It was deep—like the person was really heavy, or they hit the ground with a lot of force. The kind of force it takes to jump an eight-foot fence. My whole body went cold.

"Guys?" I turned around slowly. I could tell by their faces they'd both seen it.

"Are you guys messing with me?" Jeb asked. "Did you get someone to make these wolf-to-human prints to scare me from buying the property?"

"No, I swear." I held my hand up with my palm toward him. "Pinky promise and whatever."

He had an odd look on his face—a mix of fear, anger, and disappointment. "I gotta go."

He took off quickly, tripping and stumbling over the tree roots. Sophie and I followed him to the road.

When we got there, Mr. Zauber was standing next to his driveway pruning his hydrangea bush. His blue polka-dot bowtie was slightly crooked, and one of his tennis shoes was untied. His straw gardening hat sat awkwardly on his head, but he straightened it when he tipped it toward us to say hello. I tensed up, waiting for him to say something about staying off the Coopers' property, but instead, he gave us a huge smile.

"Your website looks very nice, girls," he said, grinning. "What did one lightning bug say to the other?"

Sophie and I smiled and shrugged.

"You glow, girl!" He laughed really hard at his joke.

Sophie and I laughed too, more out of relief than anything.

Mr. Zauber turned to Jeb and eyed him up and down. "I don't believe we've met."

"This is Jeb," Sophie said. "His father is Chester Scott. The one building the ski resort and destroying our town."

Mr. Zauber stopped smiling. "So, you're our mystery buyer."

Jeb gave Sophie a death glare. "No. I mean, not really. The property isn't even for sale yet."

"You're right. It's not. And you're going to have quite a battle for it. I predict that you'll lose." Mr. Zauber picked up his gardening shears. They glistened in the sun. "I see you've rented out the entire Berry Poppins Bed and Breakfast. Please tell Mary I tried to deliver her zinnias today, but a very persistent man in a gray shirt shooed me away." Mr. Zauber snapped a dead hydrangea with his gardening shears as he stared at Jeb.

Jeb took a step back. "Okay. Sure. Bye. See you around." He turned and walked up the road in long strides.

I ran and caught up with him. "Hey, sorry Sophie outed you like that."

"It's not your fault." He walked next to me down my driveway to the porch, grabbed his board, and skated away without looking back.

Well, that was that.

I plopped down on my porch steps and waited for Sophie to come get her board. Cody's toenails click-clacked against the porch as he came over and sat next to me. I threw my arm around him and buried my face in his soft fur.

Anger and resentment whirled inside me. Sophie had been mean to Jeb all afternoon. He'd never change his mind about the ski resort now. Sophie was way too intense. Sometimes, I wondered if I'd even be her friend if our families hadn't been so close. I never had a choice. I'd always been stuck with this stubborn, outspoken, dramatic sister-friend.

Jeb was awesome. I'd expected a stuck-up, spoiled Hollywood kid, and he wasn't that at all. He listened when I talked to him and actually seemed interested in the environment. I'd love to hear the music he wrote, but I never would. He'd never talk to me again. Not as long as Sophie was around. Maybe I needed to ditch her for a while. I needed some breathing room.

A couple of minutes later, she jogged toward me, smiling. "Mr. Zauber says he counted four hundred eggs and eighty caterpillars on the milkweed. That's twice as many as last week!"

The anger rose through me and bubbled over. I jumped up from the porch step. "Why did you call Jeb out in front of Cami and Mr. Zauber?"

Sophie stopped in the middle of the driveway. Her face fell. "What?"

"Nobody is supposed to know they're buying the Peak."

"Emma, the whole town saw them go into my restaurant. They blew their own cover."

"Still. It was awkward. You basically said, 'Hey, guys, say hello to your archenemy.'"

"Why are you sticking up for him? He's ruining our town, destroying the butterfly garden, killing trees, running animals out of their habitats—should I go on?"

"It's not him. It's his dad. How can we change his mind if you keep being mean to him?"

"We're not going to change his mind. You can't see that because you've been making googly eyes at him all day."

"What's that supposed to mean?"

"You know exactly what I mean! He's more likely to change *your* mind about the ski resort than we are to change *his*."

"You're just jealous because he didn't like you!" I stomped across the porch with Cody right at my heels. We went into the house, and I slammed the door.

Addie popped up from behind the living room couch so quickly, her honey-brown pigtails bounced. "You wanna see my LEGO spaceship?"

"No!" I ran up the stairs to my room, slammed the door, and fell on my bed.

Cody jumped up next to me and licked my nose. His tail thumped against my comforter as I ran my fingers through his silky fur. I was mad at Sophie, but I was mad at myself too. She was right. Stupid googly eyes. But I didn't know how to make it stop.

I got out the sketch I started on the mountain and took it to my desk. I pulled out my box of pastel pencils and worked on the monarchs. Usually, drawing relaxed me. I could get into the zone and think about colors and shading. But my mind wouldn't stop swirling. It wasn't like Sophie and I had never had a fight before. But this seemed different. We'd crossed some sort of line, and there was no going back. Jeb was never going to like her. She was never going to like Jeb, and I couldn't help that I did.

I finished the monarchs and started on the red wolf, but I couldn't remember what a red wolf looked like exactly. Cody thumped his tail against my feet. I reached down to stroke the soft fur under his chin. "You look nothing like a wolf. Let's look them up."

I typed red wolf into the search bar on my tablet so I had something to go by. They didn't look like typical wolves, more like a big coyote.

The wolf we heard couldn't have been a red wolf. The website said their tracks were only three-to-four-and-a-half-inches wide. A gray wolf's tracks were a little bigger, maybe four to five inches, but the tracks we'd seen were bigger than that. Probably six or seven inches.

I texted the picture to Cami. What kind of dog has paws this big?

Cami: ¡Vaya! Where did you find that? Those are humongous. Like, even an eighty-five pound German shepherd has two-and-a-half-inch paws.

That couldn't be right. Cami knew a lot about dogs, but that didn't make any sense. I typed, What canine has seven-inch paws into the search bar.

Werewolves.

Fear prickles ran down my back as thousands of web pages popped up about werewolves. But they were all fiction.

Cami: Hello?

My hand shook so much, it was hard to type. GTG!

Cami: K. That's a big dog. Fill me in when you can.

Even though my hand was shaking, I managed to poke out are werewolves real in the search bar. I clicked on an article about real werewolf sightings. In the 1500s, there had been trials against werewolves, kind of like the Salem witch trials. I scrolled past other gruesome stories from the 1700s, 1800s, 1900s, 1940s, and 1950s and then stopped on "recent sightings in the US."

The fear prickles got stronger, making the hairs on the back of my neck stand up.

I clicked on a link to preview a book about real dog men. Whoa. Two hundred pages of werewolf accounts in the US. The book was divided by regions. The first was the West with a map showing where the sightings were. A lot were in California, but there were several in Utah, Arizona, Wyoming, and Colorado. The stories were all similar—wailing howls, glowing eyes, deep growling, six-foot-long creatures that sometimes ran upright on two legs.

The next section was the Midwest, where there were only a couple.

I held my breath and clicked on the next one: the South. There was one in the Great Smoky Mountains. The chapter was "Toggle Road Beast Sighting." There were a bunch of sightings of what they called the "Toggle Road Beast" outside of Asheville. They described it as a huge wolf with fangs and reddish-brown hair. Five different people reported seeing the beast over a period of several months. There was a picture of a huge pawprint with a ruler next to it. It was seven inches long. Like the one we saw.

A message chimed on my tablet. The tingly sensation raced from my head to my feet, making me jump and drop my tablet on my desk. Cody must've sensed how revved up I was because he jumped up too. I scratched him behind his ears to calm him, took a deep breath to calm myself, and then checked the message.

Hey.

It was Jeb.

My stomach kickflipped. Geez. My roller-coaster emotions were going to kill me.

But Jeb!

He wasn't mad if he was texting me. I didn't know how to respond, so I stared at my tablet for a bit.

Hey, I finally typed and added a smiley face. No, that was stupid. I backspaced over it and hit Send.

Jeb: What do you know about that Zauber dude?

Me: He's really old, lived down the street from me all my life, helped my mom start the butterfly garden and the Monarch Larva Monitoring project here, takes care of flowers on the greenway, in town, and at Camp Eagle Crest. No kids. Wife makes pies for Max's. Blueberry and rhubarb are the best ones.

Jeb: Does he seem sketchy to you?

Mr. Zauber wasn't sketchy, more like unusual. He sometimes dressed and spoke kind of strangely, but it was because he was old-fashioned.

Me: No, but I guess he could seem odd if you didn't know him.

Jeb: Those prints turned from person to wolf on his farm.

Wait. Did Jeb think Mr. Zauber was a werewolf? My heart thumped fast. It was nice to know I wasn't alone in my craziness ... but Mr. Zauber? I hadn't considered this. It couldn't be. He was a sweet old man who'd lived there for years. Even if he was—and it wasn't possible—Sophie and I only recently heard howling. It didn't make sense for it to start now.

My message chimed.

Jeb: Now you think I've lost it.

Me: NO! I don't think you've lost it. I've been reading about werewolves since I got home. There're a lot of people who believe they're real and say they've seen them. I just can't imagine Mr. Zauber being a werewolf.

Jeb: He kind of growled at me.

Me: He's mad about the ski resort. He's usually nice to everyone. But, you're right, there was something about him that was a little off. He's usually very proper. I've never seen him with his shirt untucked or his shoelaces untied.

Jeb: Maybe that's because he'd been running down the path, jumped over the fence, and had to put his clothes on fast.

Me: No, if you knew him, you wouldn't think that. But maybe he's hiding something.

There was a knock on my door, and I jumped again. My nerves were shot.

Me: GTG! TTYL!

I sat my tablet down and grabbed my pencil. I wasn't sure why, but I felt like I needed to keep my friendship with Jeb a secret. "Yeah?"

It was Mom. She still had on her science professor clothes. She usually wore jeans and T-shirts around the house, but when she taught at UA, she dressed the part. Today, she had on a blue short-sleeved mock neck sweater with a butterfly brooch pinned below her collar bone. She always wore a brooch. She didn't get the memo that it wasn't the 1950s anymore.

Cody got up and greeted her with a tail wag. Mom leaned down and pet his head. "We're having Max's barbecue and one of Mrs. Zauber's magical blueberry pies for supper." She walked over to see what I'd drawn.

"I'm surprised Dad will go into Max's. He was pretty mad this morning," I said.

"He didn't. Zac delivered it for us." She picked up my drawing, examining it. "This is good. The wolf looks so sad. Is she a symbol of how the town feels about the ski resort?"

"Umm ... yeah, I guess. Not everybody's against it though. Like Max. Will he and Dad stop being friends?"

"Oh, no. Your dad and Max are like brothers. They've fought lots of times. Once, they actually got in a knock-down, drag-out fight over Erin McKinley—Erin Walters now. They both wanted to take her to homecoming freshman year."

"Dad dated bookstore Erin?"

"No, she went with Paul Cooper. Neither one of them was cool enough for Erin." Mom laughed and set my drawing back down on my desk.

"I guess they worked it out." I tried to laugh, but it came out a weak whimper.

"Yes. They worked through that fight and a lot of others. Every friendship has its rocky places. When you care about somebody, you work through them, and life goes on. This will be the same." She studied my face for a second. "Is everything okay?"

Tears welled up in my eyes. I wanted to tell her everything, but my feelings were so mixed up inside me, I couldn't put them into words. "Sophie and I got into a fight," I blurted out.

Mom rubbed her hand in circles on my back. "You guys are like Max and your dad. You're like sisters. You'll work it out."

"But I'm not sure if I want to. She can be so hard sometimes." I blinked back tears.

"You've always been a good friend to Sophie." Mom squeezed my shoulder. "She's not always aware of how she comes across. Give it some time."

I was relieved she didn't lecture me about loyalty and friendship to make me feel guilty. If Mom were a color, she'd be the shade after violet—a mix of intense blue and powerful but invisible ultraviolet. She always worked hard for our family, flying under the radar, doing everything she could to keep us all safe and happy.

But even with all her supermom powers, she was no match for a werewolf.

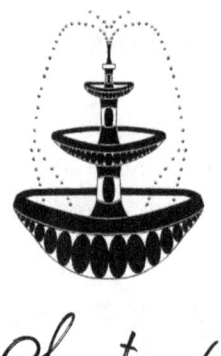

Chapter 6

Emphasis: What is the most important part of the artwork? That is where the eye should focus.

After supper, I went back to my room to read up on werewolves. When I'd added "hype up the supernatural" on my list of ways to fight the ski resort, I thought it'd be mostly hype like the ghost tours in town—a little fact, a little fiction, and just enough maybe-it-could-be-true to keep it scary. This was a whole different animal. Literally. I needed a new plan.

When I opened my tablet, there was another text from Jeb. If I played this right, it could end the ski resort. He and his dad wouldn't buy land with a bloodthirsty werewolf on it.

Jeb: You want to meet up and talk about our ww theory? We could skate too.

Whoa. My supper rolled around in my stomach. My cheeks went red hot. I had to get control of my emotions. I had a job to do, and I couldn't keep acting like a whacked-out fangirl. I needed to think of something cold to calm the fire in my face. Last week, Sophie had sent me a really funny YouTube link of Adélie penguins. I pictured myself waddling and hopping on the frozen Antarctic shore.

It worked. Sort of.

Me: Sure. Meet me in my driveway?

Jeb: coolio

Me: see you soon

Wowza. Wowza.

My tablet chimed. It was a text from Sophie. I flicked it up without reading it. I didn't have time for her drama right now.

I checked the mirror. Face still red, hair sticking up, lips chapped. Ugh. I redid my ponytail, put on lip balm, and pictured penguins sliding down snowbanks. Little tuxedoed dudes flopped over on their bellies, fins out with legs pushing through the cold snow. Once my face returned to its normal color, I told Mom I was going out, grabbed my board, and skated around the drive, waiting for Jeb.

He came flying around the corner and did a kickflip. His board and my stomach spun around in a three-sixty. My face went hot again. I imagined more penguins waddling on the snow. Penguins sliding on the ice. Penguins jumping in the cold, ice-filled water.

As Jeb slowed down, he raised his front foot and scooped the tail of his board with his back foot. The board spun again but this time lengthwise. He came to a stop right in front of me and flipped his board up into his hand. He was wearing a forest-green baseball hat that made the green in his eyes pop. He also had a huge smile—like he was happy to see me. It was super nice after my fight with Sophie.

I didn't have control of my face. My mouth was stuck in what had to look like a wide, creepy grin, and my cheeks were burning. Penguins, penguins, penguins, penguins.

"Thanks for not thinking I was crazy," he said.

"About the werewolf stuff?" Normal voice. I breathed a sigh of relief.

"Yep."

"If you're crazy, I'm crazy." Okay. Good. I sounded cool and in control of myself. Thank you, little penguins.

He laughed, then got serious. "What are we gonna do?"

"Tomorrow, I'm gonna go to the used bookstore in town to see if I can find anything written about the Toggle Road Beast."

"What's the Toggle Road Beast?"

"I read about it online in a book about dog men. It was a huge wolf spotted not far from here years ago."

"Where?" Jeb looked around like it was going to jump out of the woods any minute. He seemed awfully skittish for someone who said he wasn't scared of "supernatural crap."

"Toggle Road is about ten miles from here, near Asheville. The people who spotted it saw huge paw prints first like we did. There's no way those prints were from a red wolf or a coyote. They're way bigger."

"I looked it up too. That howl was definitely a wolf, not a coyote. It sounded different than the wolves in the video I listened to though." Jeb's eyes were wide.

"Deeper?"

He nodded slowly. "Yeah."

"That's what I thought."

"What happened to the Toggle Road Beast?" Jeb asked.

"I don't know. I could only read a little bit of the book online. If Erin doesn't have anything, I found one we can order from Canada. But it'll take five to seven days. That's way too long."

"Let's go to the bookstore now." He dropped his board and hopped on.

"Hold on. Let me double-check with my mom. I told her we'd be in the driveway." I shot a text to Mom while Jeb tick-tacked around me, smiling. I still couldn't get my face to smile normally. I avoided eye contact by keeping my eyes on my phone, waiting for her reply. Finally, it dinged. "She said it's fine as long as I get home around nine o'clock."

"Coolio. I'll follow you."

I grabbed my board with my foot, hopped on, and took off out of my driveway.

We slowed down and turned onto the greenway.

"What tricks can you do?" Jeb asked.

"None very well."

"You want me to show you some?"

"Sure."

"You can use my board if you want. It'll be easier than on your longboard." Jeb had a shortboard. The deck was wider than my longboard, but the board was shorter. The kicktail was higher—better for tricks.

We stopped at trail marker four. He smiled and rolled his board over to me. "This is a big deal. I usually don't let people use my board."

"Your girlfriend doesn't skateboard?" I stopped his board with my foot.

"My what—oh. I don't have a girlfriend. I just said that." The tops of his ears turned tomato-red.

"Why did you … that's … uh, I mean … okay. Great." My words spilled out in a tumbled, giggling mess. My face got really hot. I could feel the redness start at my neck and crawl up to my hairline. I probably had red blotches all over my face. Penguins! Penguins jumping off the ice into the cold, cold, water.

Jeb laughed too. With me, not at me, I guessed. But actually, I was kind of laughing at me, so maybe he was too.

But wait. He didn't have a girlfriend. My whole body went into overdrive like I'd been skating up the mountain. My heart raced. My chest got tight. The air got stuck in my lungs.

Penguins! Penguins! Penguins!

"Anyway. Try it out." He stood in front of me, smiling like he hadn't even noticed I was in complete freak-out mode.

But his face was red too.

I hopped on his board. The wheels were super smooth but less bouncy and harder than my board. I put everything else out of my mind and focused on skating. It took me a minute to get used to his board, but once I did, I loved it.

"What do you wanna learn?" he asked.

"An ollie."

"Nice. All you do is put your front foot in the middle of the board and the ball of your back foot on the middle of the tail. Like this." He stood on my board. "Now, to get off the ground, push down on the tail in a *pop*." He pushed down in slow motion. "As soon as the tail hits the ground, you're gonna jump up and slide your front foot toward the nose." He didn't show me full out, but he jumped a little so I'd get the idea. "Then, when you get to the highest point, get your feet over the board to land. Make sure your feet are over the bolts of both trucks, and your body's in the center of the board." He stood still in the middle of the board so I could see the landing position. "You gotta make sure you bend your knees so you won't fall. Got it?"

Nope. "Show me."

He pushed off with his left foot to a slow roll and did a perfect ollie, getting almost three feet in the air. It was amazing, especially since he was on my long board.

"You make it look easy!"

He laughed. "It is. Go!"

I pushed off to a slow roll like he had and put the ball of my right foot in the middle of the tail. I pushed down hard. The board went up, but I didn't. It kept on flying, and I hit the ground. Luckily, I landed on my feet.

"Not a bad try. As soon as you feel the tail hit the ground, you gotta jump and slide your foot to the nose. Try again."

I tried again. Ugh. Same stupid thing.

"You've got to do it all at the exact time like this." He jumped perfectly again. "Don't get mad. Keep trying."

The next try was better. I actually got my left foot up to the nose. I came down straight but not with the board. I remembered to bend my knees, but my landing wasn't very graceful. I fell back on my butt.

"Are you okay?"

"Yeah." I was relieved he didn't laugh, but now I was really mad. I tried three more times before I almost had it.

"Nice! Remember to make sure your feet are over both trucks, and your body's in the center. I'm gonna video you this time." He pulled his phone out of his back pocket.

"No way!" I held my hands up in front of my face.

"If you don't get it, it'll help you see what's wrong."

I shook my head.

"We'll delete if you don't like it."

I slowly put my hands down. "Fine."

I pushed off again, slid my right foot to the back of the board, and pushed the tail down as I slid my left foot up, guiding the board under my foot. I stayed in the air for a hot second, squared my body over the board with my feet over both trucks, bent my knees, and ... *wabam!* Landed perfectly! Then, I rolled into the grass and fell off.

He ran over to me. "Nice! Are you okay?"

"Yeah." I sat up, laughing. "I forgot to steer when I landed."

"You got it though."

He flopped down on the ground next to me and leaned in close. Really close. I could smell his minty shampoo. My stomach kickflipped. I was beginning to think of my stomach flip as *the Jeb*.

"Watch." He held his phone in front of me and played the video. He was right. It actually looked halfway decent. Well, until I rolled into the grass. "See? It was dope." He grinned and lightly bumped his knee on mine. "You wanna try again?"

"No," I laughed. "But thanks for teaching me." I bumped him back with my knee.

"Sure. Next year. I'll show you how to do it on a snowboard."

And just like that, the mood was killed.

For a second, I'd forgotten all about the ski resort. I didn't need to think about Adélie penguins to calm me down. All I needed to do was picture Paul's Peak frozen and treeless.

I hopped up quickly, pulling out my phone to check the time. "We should get going. The bookstore will close soon."

I had to focus on the plan and stop getting distracted. Jeb was the guy destroying Paul's Peak. He was going to bulldoze over the flowers in the butterfly garden. That was it. That was the most important thing.

Jeb stood and brushed the grass off his shorts. "Are there any bugs on me?"

I wanted to say yes to watch his reaction, but that would've been mean. "I don't see any, but you never know. Some are pretty small." I grabbed my board and skated down the trail.

Jeb frantically scanned his clothes before hopping on his board to catch up.

When we got to the bookstore, the lights were out and the sign on the door was flipped to Closed.

I sighed. "Dang it. Now what?"

Jeb pointed to the Black Mountain Creamery. "We could get ice cream. Dad and I went to that place after dinner. It's probably the best I've ever had."

"It *is* the best. The owners, Blair and Matt Geller-Williams, have the secret recipe from North Carolina State University. When I babysit their son, they let me eat all I want."

"Lucky."

We crossed the street to the creamery. But it was closed too. I peered through the window. Blair was putting the covers on the ice cream containers. I knocked. She looked up, smiled, and came to the door.

"Are you closed?" I asked.

"Never for you," Blair said, smiling. She turned to Jeb. "Hey, again. Jeb, right?"

Jeb nodded as Blair pushed the door open. The smell of peppermint and sweet cream drifted around us, pulling us in.

The dim glow from the ice cream coolers lit the room and gave the freshly mopped floor a little sparkle.

"You can have whatever you want. But it has to be to go," Blair said. "Matt and I are getting ready to mix new flavors. I've got a huge idea."

"What is it?" I asked. "It smells unbelievable."

Blair leaned in. "You know if I told you, I'd have to kill you. Top secret." Her eyes twinkled as she tried to hide her laughter. If Blair were a color, she'd be bright white like sugar or sweet cream. She splashed little bits of sweetness on everyone's day.

"You can't even tell me the flavor?"

She giggled. "Nice try. Come by tomorrow. If it works, you can be our first official taste-tester."

"Deal. Can I have a scoop of Black Mountain Rocky Road?"

"Make that two," Jeb said.

She gave us two huge scoops each in a waffle cone and sent us away. We walked down the mostly empty sidewalk, gripping our boards with one hand and holding the ice cream in the other. The sun was low in the sky, casting a golden light over the town. Soon, it would disappear behind the mountain in a blaze of magenta.

"I'll go to the bookstore tomorrow," I said as I pushed the button at the crosswalk.

"Should we sneak on the Zaubers' farm and do a little more research? We can follow those prints." Jeb's voice was steady, but his arm twitched.

Werewolf-hunting made my insides quiver too. "Sure." I steadied my voice. "But the Coopers', not the Zaubers'. It's less risky. I'll get grounded for life if I get caught on the Zaubers' farm." Although, "for life" was relative. I may not even make it out alive.

Three cars at the intersection screeched to a halt when the light changed red. The Walk sign flashed, and Jeb and I crossed.

"Okay," he said. "The Coopers' place is basically mine anyway, so it should be fine." He took a big bite of his rocky road.

Ugh. I hated when he said stuff like that. It wasn't "basically" his.

We followed the sidewalk to the entrance to the town square. The Bluegrass Ramblers must've just finished their after-dinner show because the roadies were packing up the set. A few people hung around, talking in little groups of twos and threes, but most of the crowd had left.

"You can't build a resort there with a werewolf running loose," I said quietly.

"That's why we're gonna find it."

"Then what?"

"Get rid of it."

"How?"

"I don't know. I haven't thought that far ahead."

They won't buy it. I was positive. "Let's go tomorrow night."

"Deal," Jeb said and took another bite of his ice cream.

I dropped my board and sat down on a bench. Jeb plopped down next to me. The fountain in front of us splashed and bubbled. A breeze swished the leaves.

"Hold this a second," I said, handing him my ice cream cone. I pulled out my phone and searched *how do you protect yourself from a werewolf.* "This says holy water, wolfsbane, and silver will repel werewolves, and if you shine a light through moonstone, it will put them in a trance." I set my phone down on the bench.

Jeb handed my ice cream back to me. "Can we get any of that stuff?"

"Well, wolfsbane is a flower. We sell aconite in our store. It's wolfsbane in a really low dose that's used to treat a fever and other stuff. We could crush it up, add some water, and put it in a squirt gun."

"Okay." He reached under his shirt and pulled out a chain. "This is silver. Will this work?"

"I think. I've got silver cross earrings. I'll wear them."

"Dope. What's moonstone?" Jeb asked.

"This says it's an iridescent gem with blue tones. I've seen it somewhere … wait, I think Mrs. Bearpaw sells silver necklaces with moonstone in the Cherokee Museum. I'll check tomorrow."

"Text me and let me know if you find it." He took another big bite of his waffle cone.

"Okay." I could feel myself brightening like the lightning bugs that were starting to flicker around us. Everything was falling into place. I might be able to have it all—the mountain, the garden, and Jeb's friendship.

"Coolio." He smiled. "You know, this really is the best ice cream I've ever had, and I've had *a lot*."

I nodded in agreement. It tasted chocolatey and light. I ate slowly, letting the sugary coolness melt in my mouth. It filled me with a sweet happiness.

Jeb pulled his phone out of his back pocket. "What's your Insta?"

Ugh. The brightness I'd been feeling went out. I couldn't let him see my Insta. He'd realize I was a total nerd. He'd never want to hang out again.

He studied my face. "You don't have to tell me. Are you private?"

"It's no big deal. It's only my art and pictures of stuff around Black Mountain. It's not like yours." I froze. Oh no, did I say that out loud?

Jeb grinned. "You follow me?" He clicked on his Insta and searched his followers.

"You have three hundred thousand followers. You're not gonna find me."

Please, no. Please, no.

"Emmas-art-828. Is that you? The profile says, *protect our monarchs*." He looked up at me, amused. "That's gotta be you."

Oh, no. Oh, no. I really wanted to crawl under the bench. "What's your Spotify?" I asked. "Are your songs on there?"

"You're changing the subject." He leaned closer, putting his shoulder right against mine, and held his phone in front of me.

I could smell his minty shampoo again, this time mixed with a hint of waffle cone. It was hard to concentrate on what he was saying. "So, Jeb360 is more real—where my actual friends are." He leaned next to me and pointed at his phone with his pinky. "I mostly post skating and snowboarding stuff and, you know, the normal travel pics and hanging out pics."

Nothing was normal at all. He traveled everywhere. Switzerland. France. Italy. His "hanging out pics" were in huge houses with walls of windows overlooking cities, beaches, and mountains, or of him sitting beside pools with splashing waterfalls where pretty girls and hot guys floated around on brightly colored pool floats.

Mine wasn't normal either, but where his was above normal, mine was far below. Just goofball me and Sophie planting flowers in the dirt, getting excited about butterfly larva, and hosting meetups in my backyard for the Environmental club. For some reason, Jeb thought I was cool enough to hang with. One look at my Instagram would dispel that belief. Not only would it be completely embarrassing, it would jeopardize my plan.

"Hello, are you listening?"

"Yeah, sorry. Your waffle cone is dripping."

"Oh, thanks." He handed me his phone and leaned forward on the bench with his waffle cone in front of him. He shoved the rest of it in his mouth and then licked his fingers. "I'm gonna request a follow, and you can follow me back if you want." He wiped his hands on his pants and took his phone back from me.

"Okay." I left my phone on the bench and kept eating my ice cream.

"You don't want me to see your art?"

"That's not it."

"I know you draw, but do you paint and do other stuff?"

"Yeah."

"What do you like the best?"

"It depends on the subject."

"Like if you were doing the fountain. Would you draw it or paint it?"

I sat quietly for a moment, watching the water bubble up and splash down. "I'd draw it with charcoal, so I could get the shadows and the way the light bounces off the water drops splashing. That's what I'd want to emphasize. That's the most beautiful part. Especially in this light."

Jeb nodded. "They're sparkling."

"Yeah."

Thankfully, he didn't ask me about my Instagram anymore. We spent the next few minutes talking about LA, the quietness of Black Mountain, and how beautiful the mountains were. He still didn't realize that the ski resort would ruin everything he loved about being here.

Sophie thought he was more likely to change my mind about the ski resort than I was to change his, but it wasn't true. If I painted this whole crazy day on one canvas, the focus wouldn't be on meeting Jeb. It would be on losing Paul's Peak and the monarch garden. That's what I would emphasize. Sure, Jeb was cute and really nice, but the garden and the peak were more important. Sophie didn't believe I'd remember that, but I would.

We sat there so long, I didn't notice it was almost dark until the ghost trolley tour pulled up on the other side of the square. Tourists spilled out and stared in our direction.

"Do they recognize me?" Jeb pulled his hat down.

"No, that's the ghost tour. They're looking at the fountain. It's haunted by—"

Jeb held up his hand. "I don't wanna know. Let's get out of here."

The clock on the courthouse struck nine, keeping the beat for the crickets and katydids as they chirped their night songs. The streetlights shimmered on the water droplets bouncing into the fountain. We picked up our boards and headed back to my house.

Chapter 7

Balance: when the elements of design are arranged symmetrically to create the impression of equal weight. Unbalanced artwork creates a sense of unease.

The next morning, I rode with Dad into town. It looked like someone had taken a picture of Black Mountain and put a gray filter on it. The hazy gray sky blocked out the mountains, the leaves were dull, and the signs and awnings over the storefronts seemed flat and colorless. It also smelled like wet mud.

We picked up the flyers and posters from the print shop. Dad seemed hopeful. He gushed about how well everything had turned out and what a good artist I was. I smiled along, but inside, I felt as gray and dreary as the weather. Sophie was meeting me at the hardware store. We were going around to the downtown stores to hang posters and leave flyers. We hadn't talked since our fight. Part of me hoped she wouldn't show.

Nobody was out in town yet. The bookstore sign was still flipped to Closed, and the windows of Matt and Blair's apartment above the creamery were shut. The light was on in Antonia's, but she must've been in the back. Max's Diner was open. Sophie sat at the counter with her back to the window, and Max stood next to her. He and Dad looked at each other, but neither waved like they usually did.

Dad unlocked the door to the store. It always seemed creepy when it was empty and dark. The old fortune-telling machine that sat by the front door was shaking, as if someone had put a penny in and stood on its scale. I stood in the doorway, squinting in the darkness for our ghost, Eloise.

"That machine has a mind of its own," Dad said. He flicked on the lights, and it stopped shaking.

I did another quick scan for ghosts but didn't see any, so I walked over to read the fortune. The dial had stopped on *The consequences will be dire*. Great. What consequences? The building of the ski resort? Hanging out with Jeb? Fighting with Sophie? I needed something more specific.

Dad set the flyers and posters down on the counter. "We're still missing one of the dollhouse dolls," he said. "Let me know if you see it."

Great. That doll could be anywhere. Eloise was very creative in her hiding spots. "You'll know by my screaming. Those dolls are creepy. I'm just gonna wait right here."

He walked through the store, flipping on more lights and revealing jampacked rows of pots and pans, souvenirs, T-shirts, toys, candy, cream soda, cards, honey, shampoo, cameras, art supplies, tools, seeds, gardening stuff, camping equipment, hiking supplies, fishing poles and lures, and keys, but no dollhouse doll.

When all the lights were on, I went to the pain-reliever section and found the aconite next to the aspirin. It was in a little tube of thirty capsules. That should be strong enough to make our wolfsbane squirt gun potion. "Hey, Dad, can I take some aconite?" I asked. "I'm … uh … working on a science project."

"Sure, just ring it up for inventory." Thankfully, he didn't ask any questions.

It wasn't really a lie. Jeb and I had a hypothesis—there was a werewolf—and a theory—aconite, a.k.a. wolfsbane, will repel it and keep us safe from bodily harm. I walked back to the front of the store, scanned it at the register, and slipped it into my backpack.

Dad made his way back to the counter. "Everybody will start opening in about ten minutes. You want to start at Erin's bookstore and work your way around the street?"

"Sure."

"Good. I'm not sure who's for the zone change and who's against it. This will be a good way to find out. Make a note of who lets you leave flyers or hang posters. If you feel up to it, you can ask some questions, get their opinions. You all can be my spies." He chuckled.

Ugh. I hadn't thought about people telling us we couldn't hang a poster. He had to be wrong. Everyone loved the garden.

Dad studied my face. "You okay?"

I shrugged. There was so much I wanted to tell him—about fighting with Sophie, about Jeb, about Mr. Zauber, about all the creepy stuff in Black Mountain—but I didn't.

Sophie came into the store and grabbed the flyers without saying hello. My stomach sank. Classic Sophie. She was going to be mad and sulky all day, punishing me for calling her out. I said goodbye to Dad, picked up the posters, and followed her out into the gray street.

Cami stood by the door with her dark curly hair pulled up in a high ponytail and wearing a blue T-shirt that said, *Cami Suárez: PetSitterExtradanaria.com*. She held a little white Chihuahua.

"Why did you bring Finnigan?" I reached up to pet him but pulled my hand back when he barked. "You can't take him in stores."

"Not true. Some stores are dog friendly."

"But he barks at everyone," Sophie said. "No one is going to take a flyer if a dog is snapping at their toes." She sounded a little snappy herself.

"I had no choice. He was already scheduled." Cami gave him a little squeeze and put her mouth by his ear. "Ignore them. You're a sweet boy. Yes, you are," she baby-talked.

"What about Carlos, Cami? Is he coming?" Sophie asked.

"He's got soccer practice."

"Great," Sophie said. "How are we going to go to every store if Evelyn and Carlos are not here, and you've got Mr. Yippy?"

I reached up—slower this time—to pet the little dog again, but he wasn't having it. "I thought Evelyn was coming with you, Cami."

"We dropped her off at the dance studio," Sophie said. "She has to help with Princess Camp because Lena's sick. She gets to be Cinderella."

Dropped her off? Evelyn lived on the other side of town from Sophie. Cami lived closer. Wait. Did Sophie and Evelyn have a sleepover without inviting me? Evelyn had only lived in Black Mountain since January. When did they become sleepover-worthy friends? "How—"

"By the way," Cami interrupted, "his name's not Mr. Yippy. It's Finnigan. Don't be mean, Sophie. You'll hurt his feelings." Cami squeezed him again and made little kissy sounds before she set him in her dog carrier bag.

Sophie rolled her eyes and gave a dramatic sigh. She was full-on Grumpy Sophie today. It was better to ignore her and plow ahead when she was like this. Besides, she and Evelyn can have sleepovers if they want. I mean, they were in the school musical together and took ballet together every Monday and Tuesday, so it made sense. It didn't bother me at all. At least, not that much. Okay, it did bother me, but I wasn't going to show it.

I turned to Cami and shrugged. "Let's start at Erin's bookstore. It's definitely dog friendly."

As we waited at the crosswalk, I tried to make the best of it and thaw Sophie's icy mood. "Did you know our dads got into a fight in high school because they both wanted to take Erin to homecoming?" I laughed.

"I doubt that. My parents started dating in high school." The iciness in her voice shot out and stopped me cold. She yanked open the door to the bookstore, sending the attached bell into a ringing frenzy.

Erin's Labrador retriever, Scout, jumped awake from her spot by the counter. She barked, and Finnigan barked back. But when Scout recognized us, she ran and jumped on me. I sat on the floor and let her crawl on my lap. Her fur was soft and warm.

Erin smiled when we came in. It took over her whole face, from her bright green eyes to her perfectly detailed eyebrows. I know why our dads fought over her in high school. She was beautiful and as nice as she was pretty. If she were a color, she'd be a soothing, iridescent forest green—like the color of the underside of a leaf when the warm sun shines through.

Her bookstore was small, but she used every bit of space. Books climbed the walls from the floor to the ceiling, and smaller shelves sat in rows through the middle. My favorite thing was the way she grouped all the books within each section by the color of their spine. It looked like a rainbow of books. They were all used, so it smelled like my granddad's attic.

Erin reached under the counter and pulled out a huge book. "Emma, I'm so glad you stopped by. This came in yesterday. It's from the San Francisco Museum of Modern Art. Looks almost brand new."

Erin had been helping me with my collection. I had books from the National Gallery of Art in Washington DC, the Met in NYC, the Art Institute of Chicago, and the National Gallery of Art, London. I've never been to any of those places, but with those books, I felt like I had.

I wiggled out from underneath Scout and took the book from Erin. It was gorgeous and smelled new. I really wanted to flop down in one of her comfy chairs and look at it, but instead, I flipped through pages quickly. "This is amazing. Thanks!"

"I haven't gotten anything new in the science section, Sophie," Erin said. "Or anything new about dogs, Camilia. Although, I think you're a dog expert by now."

Cami sat down next to Scout and put Finnigan on her lap. The dogs sniffed each other. "That's okay. We don't have time to read anyway. We're helping Emma's dad fight the ski resort."

"Awesome. What are you doing? I want to help too." Her voice was soothing and warm like the summer sun. It warmed me from the inside out.

I held up the posters. "Can you hang these and sign our petition?"

"Absolutely!" Erin adjusted her chestnut ponytail, got tape out of the desk drawer, and hung a poster on her window. She placed a stack of flyers on the counter, and then we helped her hang some around the bookshelves.

I hung back in the fantasy section, skimming the titles.

"Are you looking for anything in particular?" Erin asked.

"Do you have any books about werewolves?" I paused, then added, "Like accounts where people believe they saw a real werewolf?"

"Actually, I do. Over here in the Strange but True Tales section." Erin laughed. "Between you and me, these stories are definitely strange but probably not true."

She led me to a shelf that had dozens of books about supernatural activities. A lot of them were local. There were *Ghosts of Black Mountain*, *Ghost Tales of Asheville*, and *The Haunting of the Biltmore*. Erin pulled two books off the shelf and handed them to me. One I'd seen online, *Real Dog Men of America*—that was super lucky; it would've taken so long to ship it—and another one was *The Beast on Toggle Road*. I couldn't believe it! They were a little beat up and smelled old, but they were perfect. "I'll take both."

Sophie stood by the door with her hands on her hips. "What are you getting those for?"

"This one's about strange wolf sightings not far from us."

"So?"

"So ..." My mind raced to think of a good answer. She still thought the prints were from an actual wolf. "You know what Miss Bettie said yesterday about scaring people away with supernatural stories? I'm getting books for research."

Erin nodded. "I remember when the Toggle Road incident happened. People claimed they saw things around here too, not too far from your house, Emma. That summer, our parents wouldn't let us out past dark."

"What happened?"

"Willa Cooper found huge paw prints in her yard near Black Mountain Road. Then, people claimed they heard howling. The Coopers did and someone else. I don't remember who. Maybe the Zaubers? Anyway, Willa and some other kids camped out one night with a camera. They heard howling, went to investigate, and got so scared, they all ran home. They claimed they saw the Toggle Road Beast. It was a huge wolf-like creature with fangs and long sharp claws."

Whoa. The hair on my arms stood up. Cami stared at me, eyes wide.

Sophie rolled her eyes and tapped her foot impatiently. "Nobody's going to believe that now, Emma. We need to focus on science, not science fiction. The facts will help us get everybody on our side."

Sophie would never believe it, but this sounded like proof to me. The Toggle Road Beast was back. It had to be.

Erin stuck a stray hair behind her ear. "Paul told me it was all made up. They didn't actually see anything."

After what I'd seen and heard, I doubted they'd made it up. I needed to talk to Willa. "It makes a good story, though," I said. "That's the kind of stuff people latch on to."

"People were definitely freaked out for a while. Then it all died down," Erin said.

I pulled my birthday money out of my pocket. "I'll take both books."

She smiled. "You can have them. It'll be my contribution to your cause."

I hugged her thank you and stuffed the books into my backpack.

As we headed to the door, Scout ran over and leaned her head on me. I leaned down and hugged her too.

"You're getting too distracted," Sophie said after the door closed behind us. "First Jeb and now werewolves."

The sticky, muggy day didn't seem to be stopping Sophie the Snow Queen.

"Come on Sophie, don't you think it's weird that we heard howling and saw that huge footprint like the Coopers did?" She could debate "facts" all she wanted. But if someone saw the beast and heard the beast, it was a fact.

"Does this have to do with the print you sent me? Do you think that's the Toggle Road Beast?" Cami asked.

"It's a coincidence," Sophie said. "Erin said they made it up. Please, focus guys." She stomped down the sidewalk in front of us.

I turned toward Cami. "Yeah, I think the Toggle Road Beast is back. We found those prints near Paul's Peak."

Cami nodded. "Yesterday, when I was walking Poncho past the Coopers' old place, he went nuts. Well, nuttier than usual. He jumped up and started pulling on the leash. He pulled it right out of my hand and ran all the way home."

Sophie stopped in front of the antique store and gave Cami a side-eye. "That means nothing, Cami. Poncho is always trying to get away from you." She pulled open the door, hitting us with the bitter smell of furniture polish and musty couches.

Before we could even walk in, Mr. Smith shook his head. "Sorry, girls. No flyers in here."

"You're not supporting our fight against the ski resort?" I realized my mouth had dropped open, so I closed it.

"It's not personal, girls. That ski resort will bring in a lot more tourists, which means more business. It's purely economics."

"But the garden brings in tourists." I kept my voice pleasant, but I could feel the anger welling up.

"Yeah," Cami said. "Skiers aren't going to buy antiques, Mr. Smith. Only old people want this stuff. Old people don't ski, but they love flowers and butterflies." Cami had a point.

"Sorry, girls. It's a no. Please, close the door. It's getting hot out there."

His service dog, Roscoe, looked up at us and wagged his tail. Finnigan gave him a little yip as Sophie let the door shut.

We stared at each other in disbelief. Dad said some people would be against it, but I hadn't actually believed him.

Mrs. Patterson's jewelry store was next door. She'd almost passed out when she saw Chester yesterday, so after hearing Mr. Smith say no, I seriously doubted she'd be a yes. But we decided to try anyway.

As soon as we stepped in through the door, Finnigan went nuts. He barked and squirmed in Cami's arms until he broke free and leaped to the ground. He barked like a maniac, circling the store. Cami chased behind him. I tried to get in front of him and catch him, but he zoomed between my legs. He ran behind the counter and flushed out Mrs. Patterson's cat, who jumped on the jewelry case.

"Get that dog out of here!" Mrs. Patterson yelled. Her voice was high and pitchy as she tried to make herself heard over Finnigan's barking and the cat's hissing.

Cami crawled under the counter and waved a dog treat. Finnigan looked back and forth between Cami and the cat, like he was weighing his options. Finally, he ran to Cami. She gave him the treat, scooped him up, and crawled back out from under the counter.

Sophie shot death glares at Cami as she carried Finnigan out the door. "I'm so sorry, Mrs. Patterson," Sophie said, holding up a flyer. "Would you be interested in putting these on your counter?" Her voice cracked.

"You've got to be kidding, right?" Mrs. Patterson picked up her cat and cuddled it under her chin. "You want to keep Chester Scott from moving back?"

"Umm … we don't have anything against Chester," I said and held up the poster of the meadow. "We just don't want him to build his resort here."

"Well, I want him to. We go way back. My cousin, Barbra, used to babysit for him. I'm pretty sure I met him when I was a kid." She kissed the cat on top of its head and set it down on the floor. "And please, remember: no dogs allowed!"

"I'm really sorry, Mrs. Patterson. We will." Sophie pushed open the door and walked up to Cami on the sidewalk. "You've got to do something with that dog," Sophie said. "He's a nuisance."

Cami put Finnigan in her carrier bag, and we went to Mrs. Hartford's art supply shop next. My three favorite places in Black Mountain were Paul's Peak, the butterfly garden, and Little Wing Hollow Art Supply Store and Gallery. Just walking in lifted my mood.

Mrs. Hartford had every art supply I could ever want. I'd spent hours walking down aisles, looking at supplies, touching smooth paper, and breathing in the sweet smell of possibility. Paper, pens, paints, pastels, pencils, markers, glue—everything just waiting to be something else. To be whatever I wanted it to be.

It was always busy. Even this morning, five girls—two in UNC Asheville T-shirts—stood in the paper section, talking excitingly about brown sketchbook paper. A lady in a long green sweater and sandals picked through the oil paints, and an older couple leaned in close to each other, whispering in the small gallery in the back. Carlos Suárez, Cami's brother, who was also in my Saturday afternoon art class, was doodling on the practice pad with the alcohol markers.

Mrs. Hartford lit up when she saw me. Like, literally. Not only did her dark-brown face glow, but her orange and pink silky duster seemed more intense. "Emma! How's my favorite student?" Her brown eyes twinkled behind her purple glasses. If she were a color, she'd be purple like her glasses—regal and stately like a queen but also fun and tricky like the royal jester.

Carlos's head jerked toward us. "Hey! You said I was your favorite." He laughed.

"You're no one's favorite, you loser," Cami said, laughing.

"Sorry, Camilia," Mrs. Hartford said. "No dogs in here."

"Yeah, get lost. Hasta luego, loser," Carlos said.

"*You* get lost." Cami went back out the door as Finnigan barked at the girls in the UNC Asheville T-shirts.

"Carlos, why aren't you helping us?" Sophie waved the flyers in front of him. "We've got a ton of stores to go to, and it's basically just me and Emma since your sister brought that annoying dog."

"Currently on my way to practice." He rolled a soccer ball out into the aisle with his left foot and then dribbled it over to his right. "I came in to get a new red marker. Mine ran out. I don't wanna get behind. Gotta keep locked into my favorite student status, right, Mrs. Hartford?"

"You know all of you are my favorites," Mrs. Hartford said, winking. "Except that dog." Her gold hoop earrings swayed, and her floral duster floated around her as she walked toward me and Sophie.

"But I really am your favorite." I laughed too.

"That depends." She smiled. "How far are you in your art journal? Carlos has six pages of terms already. He's going to experiment with alcohol markers to show balance." Her bracelets clanged as she gestured toward Carlos.

Carlos flipped open his sketchbook and held it up. He'd drawn vivid shapes, like a kaleidoscope. It was perfectly symmetrical.

"Nice." I smiled. "I've done six terms too. Also, this." I held up my poster of the meadow.

Carlos pushed his black hair out of his eyes. "You drew that last year."

"Right. Okay, then. This." I held up the poster with the monarch.

"Go off!" Carlos beat two markers on the pad like he was playing drums. He hit the rack with a marker like it was a cymbal. "That's intense!"

"Thanks," I said, laughing. "I'm using it for the art journal for the term *intensity*."

"Lovely, Emma. Shall I hang it in the window?" Mrs. Hartford asked.

"Please."

"Could you also put some of these flyers on the counter?" Sophie held a stack out to Mrs. Hartford, who smiled as she took them. "And sign our petition? There's a link on our website."

"Absolutely. We can't have our garden destroyed. Where would we have our plein air painting lessons?"

"Thank you so much, Mrs. Hartford! Hasta luego, Carlos." I turned toward the door.

"Keep working on that journal," Mrs. Hartford called behind me. "You're a gifted artist with natural talent. You need to learn the why behind the what so you can tackle all those AP classes in high school."

"Yes, ma'am!"

We stepped out of the air-conditioned art store into the heat and found Cami sitting on a bench in the shade. Finnigan was under her feet, drinking some water out of a pop-up travel bowl.

Dogs weren't allowed in the clothing store, so Sophie and I bopped in without Cami and Finnigan. They were a yes.

The quilt shop was a no.

Cami stayed on the bench while Sophie and I went down the alley behind the quilt shop. The gray clouds pushed down over us, and the buildings blocked the breeze, making it stuffy and hot. Even the flowers in front of the Black Mountain Museum of the Cherokee looked tired and wilted.

The museum had been started by Stella Bearpaw with donations and money she'd made selling jewelry and crafts. Small and cramped and a little dark, it had all kinds of cool stuff, like authentic Cherokee pottery and baskets, some old carved stones that were once used as tools, a bunch of arrowheads, and her prized possession: an ancient mask carved out of wood that looked like a wolf. It had been made by one of her ancestors.

She'd definitely be a yes.

She'd commissioned a piece from me a few weeks ago. It hung over a model of the Great Smoky mountains. She asked me to paint *Our Creator put us here to care for and protect this land* and add a bunch of flowers and butterflies around the border.

She understood.

"Ahh, my favorite girls," she said when we stepped inside. Her face crinkled in a huge smile, and her gray hair poked out under a blue bandanna. "What do you have for me?"

I held up my posters, and she oohed at my artwork before sitting the flyers on the counter and choosing a poster to hang by the Trail of Tears display.

While Sophie helped her hang the poster, I turned the necklace rack slowly, searching for moonstone. She had moonstone rings, but I needed something bigger. I kept turning until I saw what I needed—a big hunk of iridescent blue moonstone dangling from a long silver chain. I lifted it off the display and held the stone in front of me. "This is gorgeous," I said as I pulled my birthday money out of my pocket. "I'll take it."

"Good choice." Mrs. Bearpaw met me at the counter and scanned the necklace. "Moonstone has positive energy." She held the stone to the light and turned it. "See the specks of gold, blue, and purple?"

I nodded.

"When the moon cycles, it connects us to the ebb and flow of our lives. This stone will help you channel your feminine potential." She smiled and met my eyes. "You are a powerful girl. When you wear this, you'll be reminded that you can do anything." She gently placed the necklace around my neck.

I felt like the chosen one in a superhero movie, as if the necklace had some sort of hidden power. "Thank you so much."

On the way out, I paused by the wolf mask. "Mrs. Bearpaw, are there any Cherokee stories about werewolves?"

"Hmm. Not werewolves, exactly. Let's see." She put on her reading glasses and pulled a folder out from under the counter. She flipped through some papers. "Here, you can have this," she said, handing me one. "This documents the Cherokee names of local areas. She pointed to a section. *"Gili-Dinehun'yi,* an English phonemic interpretation of the Cherokee word, means *where the dogs live*. It's up near you by the Swannanoa River, named for two large red dogs that were once seen on the bank."

"No way! When did they name it that?"

"Well, archaeologists can date Cherokee back at least twelve thousand years, but we believe we've been here longer."

Sophie looked bright and excited. "You think they might've been red wolves?"

My brain swirled like the rapids in the river. They'd been werewolves. I was sure. There'd been werewolves in Black Mountain for hundreds, maybe thousands of years. This proved it!

Mrs. Bearpaw shrugged. "Red wolves or wolf-shifters. Who knows? Maybe they're the same." Her eyes twinkled behind her reading glasses. "You decide."

Shapeshifters. That was something I hadn't considered. "What's the difference between a werewolf and a wolf-shifter?" I asked.

Mrs. Bearpaw smiled. "Very good question. It's my understanding that in folklore, a werewolf is a vicious beast that transforms from man to wolf on the night of a full moon. It isn't able to control its transformation. Once it becomes a wolf, it goes on a vicious rampage and destroys everything it comes across. Right?"

I nodded. Sophie sighed loudly.

"But a wolf-shifter changes at will, and most importantly, it's not a random killer but a protector."

Whoa. "A protector?"

"Yes, in Cherokee legend, a wolf spirit possesses a person and transforms them. But unlike werewolves, this wolf is a protector made by the Great Creator to protect us from threats."

Like people who wanted to destroy the forest and the butterfly garden. Maybe the prints we'd seen belonged to a wolf-shifter, not a werewolf. Would that make it less dangerous? I put the paper in my backpack to read later.

Chapter 8

Space: the distance around and between forms

The news about the red dogs didn't help Sophie's mood like I'd hoped. She and the sky refused to be anything but gray. We trudged down the sidewalk under the shops' dull awnings and through their swinging doors. The cupcake bakery, coffee house, jewelry store, and clock shop were all nos, but the music store and honey store let us hang posters in their windows. So far, it was more nos than yesses. This was going to be a hard fight. I had no idea people were so selfish and shortsighted. My hope sunk with every no, and along with it, my mood. On top of that, Sophie annoyed the heck out of me. Inside the shops, she flashed her smile and spread her charm, but when we were outside she barely spoke to me.

I focused on the moonstone swinging around my neck. It was like a happy little beam of light. Mrs. Bearpaw was right. It made me feel powerful. I pictured Sophie as the Snow Queen trying to freeze me with her icy mood, but instead, I shattered that negative vibe into bits with warm summer moonlight.

We met up with Cami in the town square and handed flyers to people as they walked by or sat in rocking chairs. Some of the tourists asked directions to the greenway trail, and some wanted to know more about monarchs. The sidewalk became more crowded as the day went on. Cami carried Finnigan and kept giving him treats to keep him from barking. She was only a little successful.

At lunchtime, the crowd flocked to the restaurants. The street smelled like hot bread, tangy oregano, and warm tomato sauce, making my stomach rumble. We followed the heavenly scents to Antonia's, where we found Evelyn outside saving us a table. Her legs stretched out onto a chair, and her dance bag sat in another one. She still had her tiara on. It glittered in front of her high bun.

"Why you looking so mad, Soph? I came as soon as I could." She sat up straight and moved her bag so we could sit.

"She's mad at me, not you," I said, plopping down into a chair.

"No, she's mad at me for bringing Finnigan." Cami sat down next to me and put the dog in her lap.

"Guys." Sophie stood with her hands on her hips. "I'm not mad at anyone." Total lie. She was probably mad at all of us. "How was dance camp?" She made her voice sound soft and sweet.

"Fun. But at first, those little kids told me I don't look like Cinderella. So, I go, 'I'm not the white, yellow-haired cartoon Cinderella. I'm the real live Black Cinderella.' I showed them a clip of Brandy and Whitney singing *Impossible/Possible*. You know, from that live action one from the '90s?"

I nodded. "That's the best one."

She beamed. "Sure is. They said I looked like Brandy. They think I'm famous now." She laughed.

We all laughed too.

"You should revive that on Broadway someday, with diversity like that," I said.

"I think I will. Watch out, New York City! Evelyn Williams is coming."

She probably would too. Evelyn did anything she set her mind to. She was a persistent but pleasant royal blue.

Sophie handed Evelyn some flyers, and Cami and Finnigan waited outside while the rest of us went in.

Antonia was a yes, so I hung a poster in the window for her. Sophie set the flyers on the counter, and Evelyn handed a few to the people in line. We ordered sandwiches to go and went back outside to sit with Cami and Finnigan, who had finally worn himself out. He slept under the table.

I finally had a chance to fill Cami in on everything Mrs. Bearpaw had said about the red dogs. Her eyes got wider and wider as I talked. "That sounds like the legend of Cuetlachtli," she said when I was done. "It's an old, *old* Aztec story. The guy, Cuetlachtli—his name means wolf—came from a long line of hunters who were men during the day but became wolves at night." She paused to take a drink of her Pisgah Pineapple cream soda.

"Was he friendly, or did they attack people?" I asked, then crammed some of fries in my mouth.

"Not friendly. His soldiers drank his blood so they could become wolves. They'd go into villages at night as wolves and kill people while they slept. Together, they ruled the city of El Tajín and the villages nearby for years. Eventually, he became king of the whole North."

I swallowed my fries, but it felt like they were stuck in my throat. "Wowza."

"Hold on. That's not all. Some of his followers went against him. They had a shaman use his powers to turn them into jaguars and coyotes. They had a huge battle, and a lot of them died, but Cuetlachtli vanished and reappeared in the mountains of what is now the US. After that, he was never seen again."

"Wait. The mountains like here—the Great Smokies?"

Cami nodded. "Could be. Maybe that's what those red dogs were. Descendants of Cuetlachtli."

"And maybe the Toggle Road Beast is too."

"Geez. I gotta keep my pet-sitting dogs out of the woods."

Sophie and Evelyn looked at us like we were crazy.

"Y'all don't actually believe there's a wolf beast loose in the forest, do you?" Evelyn asked as she swirled her fry in some ketchup.

Sophie laughed.

"I think anything is possible," I said.

"Show her the picture of the paw prints, Emma," Cami said. "They're huge."

Evelyn stuck her fry in her mouth and waved her hand in front of my phone. "Save yourself the trouble. I think y'all nuts. No changing my mind about that."

Sophie leaned over and whispered something to Evelyn. They both laughed.

I started to put my phone away, but instead I shot Jeb a text. He'd never laugh at me. I found the book at the bookstore and a moonstone necklace at the Cherokee museum! Can you meet up in a couple of hours?

Jeb: Awesome! Sure thing.

Me: I'll text you when I get home.

I hung back with Cami when Sophie and Evelyn got up to throw away their trash. "If we can prove to Jeb that the Toggle Road Beast is back, he'll never build here."

She nodded. "But how you gonna prove that?"

"We're going out tonight to find it."

"Estás loco. Totally nuts."

"Does that mean you don't wanna join?'

"Exacto! Descendientes de Cuetlachtli are bloodthirsty monsters. I'm not gonna go looking for one."

We threw our trash away and crossed the street to go to Black Mountain Creamery. I knew Blair and Matt would be a yes. They used ingredients from local dairy farms. A business that supported local farms would definitely be against large commercial development.

In front of the creamery, a little boy swatted at a bee that flew around his cup full of Swannanoa River Strawberry. Sophie lectured him about pollinators, and I handed his mom a flyer.

When we walked in, the smell of waffle cones and cool air surrounded us. I breathed it in and scanned the case to see if the new flavor was out yet. Usually, I taste-tested new ones but always ended up with Black Mountain Rocky Road. There wasn't a line yet, just a couple of people sitting at the little round tables and a hiker dude sitting on a stool at the counter.

Matt Geller-Reynolds was the only one working. He wore a white sweater with red stripes, black jeans, and black boots. He dressed like a guy on a fashion runway, not a guy scooping ice cream in the North Carolina mountains. If he were a color, he'd be purply-blue like his favorite flavor, Blue Ridge Blueberry—usually sweet but randomly sour.

"Hey, guys," he said and grabbed four spoons. "Today's flavor is peppermint cream." He scooped ice cream onto the spoons and handed one to each of us, then got a scoop of vanilla for Finnigan.

I held the ice cream on my tongue and let it melt slowly. As it dissolved, little pieces of peppermint stayed on my tongue. It was delicious. "It tastes like Christmas in June," I said.

"We're testing new flavors for Chester." Matt's eyes lit up. "He came yesterday and tried the Blue Ridge Blueberry. He wants us to sell our ice cream at the resort."

"So, you're for the ski resort?" Sophie turned pale. She looked like she was going to throw up peppermint cream all over Matt.

"I know what you guys are thinking—"

"How could you?" I felt sick too. "They're going to tear down the trees and destroy the butterfly garden. They'll build more roads. All that pollution will hurt us and the cows." I slammed the little spoon into the trashcan, making the lid swing back and forth.

"Your ice cream is not gonna taste the same," Evelyn said as she threw her spoon away too. "It's gonna be nasty."

"The kids aren't wrong," the guy sitting at the counter said. He looked like a lot of other hikers passing through Black Mountain—long scraggly beard with a little gray, longish hair, hiking boots, khaki shorts, and a navy-blue pullover. "There's been studies that have linked air pollution to food quality. It definitely affects it."

"Well ..." Matt scrunched up his eyebrows. "There'll be a lot of construction at first, but then it'll only be tourists. Instead of fighting Chester, you should work with him. He's super nice. I think he'll be open to your concerns."

"Ha," the guy said. "You can't trust him. He's only out for himself. He'll exploit this town and all these little businesses. You'll regret it. If that zoning gets changed, this whole town will go down the toilet."

Sophie handed the man a flyer. "We have a petition for anyone against the ski resort. The web page is on here."

"Sounds great. Thanks, kid." The guy took the flyer, folded it up, and stuck it in his pocket.

I held up my stack of posters in front of Matt. The one with the butterfly meadow was on top. "So, you probably won't hang one of these in your window."

His face softened. "That's gorgeous, Emma. Did you design that?"

I nodded.

"You're so talented. Blair and I should use you for our design work. You want to draw something for the peppermint cream container?" He smiled so big, I had to look away.

My face stung, like he'd smacked me. He was being nice about my art, but I was mad at him for not supporting us. My mixed emotions whirled around inside me. I turned and ran out the door.

I came to a quick stop on the sidewalk. The sheriff's car was parked in front of our hardware store, and Dad was walking out of the store behind Sheriff Hernandez.

As Dad climbed into the seat behind him, I sprinted over and knocked on the car's passenger side window. The sheriff rolled it down, and I leaned in. "Dad?"

"Hey, sweetie. I'm going to the station with Simon. No big deal." His hand twitched as he pushed his glasses up the bridge of his nose.

"What's no big deal?"

Sheriff Hernandez leaned over across the seat. A frown creased his forehead. "Confidential police business, Emma. We're only asking your dad some questions. He's not a suspect."

"A what?" Panic surged through me like a flash flood during a thunderstorm.

Cami ran up next to me. "Tío Simon, where are you taking Emma's dad?"

"Don't worry. He'll be back soon." Sheriff Hernandez stuck his hat on, covering his black hair.

Dad nodded and forced a smile.

"Step back, girls. I'm pulling away now." Sheriff Hernandez pushed the button to roll up the window.

I stepped back up to the sidewalk and stood next to Sophie as the car drove off.

"What's that about?" Sophie asked. The coldness in her voice had melted to concern.

I shook my head and pulled out my phone to call Mom. She didn't answer. I handed my posters to Evelyn. "You guys finish. I gotta find my mom."

I ran back across the street through the alley to take the shortcut to the greenway trail, calling Mom again as I ran. She still didn't answer. I stopped running and texted her.

Me: Mom, what's going on? The sheriff took Dad to the station.

I ran the rest of the way home. When I reached the porch, I took the steps two at a time and landed in front of the door. The floorboards creaked and moaned like they were freaking out too. I leaned down, holding the sharp stitch that had started in my side. My heart beat like it would fly right out of my chest.

My phone chimed, but it wasn't Mom's ring.

Jeb: Hey. My dad got a death threat. Now I can't go out. Not even with Tweedledum or Tweedledee.

Me: What???

Jeb sent a picture of a postcard that looked straight out of a TV crime show. The letters had been cut out of magazines. *Leave town today or leave in a body bag tomorrow*, it said.

Me: OMG!

Jeb: Creepy, right????

Me: Very. Are you leaving?

Jeb: No. Dad's mad. He's not leaving until he buys the property. Mom wants me to go back to LA, but she's not even there. She's filming in Australia. I'd be stuck alone with Tweedledum. I want to stay here.

Me: Aren't you scared?

Jeb: No.

Wait. Sheriff Hernandez had said Dad wasn't a suspect. Was this what he'd meant? But then why would they be questioning Dad?

I ran into the house. "Mom! Mom!"

Cody came running out of the kitchen, followed by Miss Bettie, who was drying her hands with a towel. "Your mama's at work. What's the matter?"

"Dad—" I couldn't get the words out. I collapsed into the soft couch cushions, and Cody jumped up next to me. I felt like Sophie when she was having one of her anxiety attacks. I took slow, deep breaths and pet Cody as I counted backward from five in my head.

Miss Bettie went into the kitchen and came back out with a glass of water. I took a long drink and set the glass on the coffee table.

"What's going on?"

"It's all a big mistake," I blurted out. "They think Dad threatened Chester Scott."

"What in the world?" Bettie's eye were wide.

I told her everything—sneaking into the diner, meeting Jeb on the greenway, hiking to Paul's Peak, Dad going to the police station, and Jeb's dad getting a death threat.

She tried to call Mom but didn't get an answer either. "There's only one thing we can do right now." She pushed herself up off the couch.

"What's that?"

"Make my famous cinnamon rolls."

"I don't want any rolls."

"You do too. Go get Addie, and y'all can help."

Bettie was right. Making rolls helped me work out my anger. She and Addie mixed the sugar, salt, and baking powder together, and I squeezed and mushed the butter into the mixture with my hands. Then, I cracked the eggs hard on the side of a bowl and beat the milk and eggs together. When it was mixed well, Addie poured it and stirred it into dough. I took the dough out and slammed it on the wax paper on the counter.

I made a fist and pounded the dough hard in the center. Little pieces of dough popped up. I mashed them down and pounded it for Sophie, who was making things way harder than they should be, and a couple of pounds for Jeb, who'd started this whole mess. I flipped it over and pounded for Matt and Blair, who should be on our side. Then I kneaded and pounded for every (*pound*) single (*pound*) business (*pound*) that'd said no (*pound, pound, pound*) to our hanging our posters.

"That's good, Emma. Let's roll it now." Miss Bettie shooed me out of the way and handed the roller to Addie.

I collapsed on the floor next to Cody, and he nudged my hand with his nose. I threw my arm around him, out of breath from all the pounding.

Miss Bettie's phone rang, making us all jump.

It was Mom. Finally! She was with Dad at the police station. They'd be on their way home soon, and she'd tell us everything.

❀ ❀ ❀

By the time they got home, the house was filled with the smell of freshly baked cinnamon rolls and the chicken pot pie Miss Bettie made for supper. Dad went directly to the kitchen and plopped a piece of cinnamon roll in his mouth.

Over supper, Mom and Dad filled us in on what had happened. The postcard was left inside the Berry Poppins Bed and Breakfast where Chester and Jeb were staying. Dad had been there in the afternoon to change the locks, so he had a key. The postcard had come from his store, and his fingerprints were on it and the doorknob. That wasn't unusual since he'd changed the locks and sold the postcard. They didn't arrest Dad, just asked him a bunch of questions.

The problem was his alibi. He'd left the house last night to walk Cody. It was only him and the dog, and they were gone for about thirty minutes. According to the police, that would have given him plenty of time to sneak into the house and leave the postcard. He was now officially a suspect. He wasn't supposed to leave town.

It didn't make sense. No way Dad would ever threaten anyone. Besides, he hadn't known Chester and Jeb were staying at Berry Poppins. He changed locks at rental places all the time in Black Mountain. It wasn't a big deal.

After we finished eating and cleaned the kitchen, I went upstairs to my room and collapsed on my bed. To distract myself, I opened my Instagram and scrolled through.

The Black Mountain Garden Club had posted a picture of Evelyn, Sophie, and Cami holding up our posters and flyers. The caption said, *Thanks to the Black Mountain Middle School Environmental Club for creating these beautiful posters and educating the community about the importance of saving our garden. Nice job, girls! You can sign the petition at no-blackmountainskiresort.com.* Okay. That was great, but where was my shout-out? I'd created the posters. They could've at least tagged me.

I kept scrolling through and stopped at a post Evelyn had made of her and Sophie. I was right. They did have a sleepover. There was a series of them roasting marshmallows in Sophie's firepit.

They were smiling and laughing, like it was the most fun they'd ever had in their lives.

Geez. Good for them. I mean, Sophie can have other friends sleep over besides me. It shouldn't make me sad. Cami had spent a whole weekend and a school night here once when her parents went to a wedding in Mexico.

But this felt all wrong. We were all friends, but before Evelyn moved here, the BFFs had been me and Sophie, Cami and Brie, and Carlos and Jayden. It's how we always split up. Well, unless people were out of town, like Brie and Jayden were now.

Was I being replaced? Over one stupid fight?

I quit scrolling and clicked on my follow requests. There was the one Jeb had sent last night. I held my finger over it.

Part of me wished I'd never met him—that he'd never even come to Black Mountain. Since he got here, everything had flipped upside down. Sophie and I were fighting. Max and Dad were fighting. Now Dad may be in big trouble—all because Jeb wanted a place to snowboard.

If Jeb were a color, he'd be gray. Not the gray you get from mixing black and white. But the primary gray you get when you mix the bright primary colors—red, yellow, and blue. He took things that were beautiful and bright and mixed them all up into a murky gray blob.

I tapped *accept* anyway. Hopefully, he'd click on the link to no-blackmountainskiresort.com and learn a few things. My finger twitched over the request button. I didn't want to follow him back … but I also kind of did. Ugh.

Wait. I'd completely forgotten we'd been texting. I pulled up my messages and there was one from two hours ago. I texted him back to see what he knew.

Me: They took my dad down to the police station. He's a suspect.

Jeb: Wait, your dad is the locksmith??

Me: Yeah, he owns the hardware store and changes locks.

Jeb: Whoa

Me: He didn't do it. He can't even kill a spider. Literally catches them on paper towels and pitches them out the back door.

Jeb: I believe you

Butterflies flitted inside my stomach. That was good. Jeb was on my side. We could find the real suspect, and I could keep trying to convince him to nix the ski resort. I wasn't giving up yet, no matter how gray he was.

Me: Let's figure out who did it. Who knows where you're staying besides me, Sophie, Mr. Zauber, and my dad? Did you have any food delivered or anything?

Jeb: Nothing delivered. The people who own this B&B know, but they signed a confidentiality agreement. They wouldn't tell anyone. It's a big-time fine if they do.

Me: That leaves Sophie and Mr. Zauber.

Jeb: My money's on Zauber

Me: It wouldn't be Sophie, for sure. But it doesn't make any sense. It can't be Mr. Zauber.

Jeb: Why not? He has more to lose than anyone. The ski resort will be right next to his property. If he's trying to hide something behind that fortress of trees, we'll see it. We're putting a fifteen-story hotel building right next door.

Dang! Fifteen stories. All the air left my body, like I'd been kickedflipped onto the hard pavement. The ski resort was going to be huge.

Me: How would he have gotten in?

Jeb: IDK. Let's skip the Coopers and go Zaubers' farm and see what we can find out.

I'd never been on Mr. Zauber's farm. He'd put the fence up years ago after Erin's brother and that girl drowned in the river. There were No Trespassing signs at the driveway and around the property on the fence. I didn't even know what was on the other side. Thick woods surrounded his farm with a lot of undergrowth. He'd lined most of the fence along the road with different kinds of flowering bushes, most of them thorny.

I shouldn't go on his farm. I knew this because I'd heard this my whole life. I knew this like I knew how to breathe and walk. But maybe we could find evidence that could clear Dad. I could hear Sophie now. *If Jeb jumped off a cliff, would you jump too?*

Evidently, I would because I typed, Let's do it. I'll text you when I'm on the way.

Jeb: Coolio

Chapter 9

Rhythm: showing movement by repeating elements.
Straight lines allow the eye to zip around quickly;
lots of the same element create a f r a n t i c feeling

I rolled off my bed and hopped around the dirty clothes, books, and art supplies lying like land mines between my bed and the door. If Mom saw my room, she'd morph into a drill sergeant and order me to clean my room ASAP. I closed the door behind me and went downstairs.

I found Mom in the kitchen with Addie and Cody. "Can I go skate on the greenway?" I asked as I leaned down and pet Cody under his chin. He lay down and rolled on his back so I could rub his belly.

"It's Wednesday night." Mom pointed to the calendar hanging by the fridge. She looked annoyed, like I was supposed to remember the days of the week when I wasn't in school. "I have class and lab. It's your night to watch Addie until Dad gets back from the store."

"Can't Miss Bettie?"

She didn't answer. Just gave me that flat Mom stare. Ugh. How was I supposed to clear Dad if I had to babysit?

Addie sat at the kitchen island with her hair in pigtails and her bare feet dangling. "We can play with my dollhouse or video games or LEGOs, or draw, or watch YouTube, or you can teach me to skateboard, or we can go to the creamery, or—"

"How about we start with eating a cinnamon roll?" I grabbed a knife out of the drawer and cut one for me and for Addie. She was magenta—bubbly and bright and always wanting to be the center of attention.

"Emma's in charge now, Addie." Mom kissed the top of her head. "I'll be back around nine thirty." She gave me a one-armed hug. "If you need anything, call your dad. He'll be home from the store around nine."

I one-arm hugged her back. "Is Dad okay?"

"Yes. I'm sure this'll blow over soon. Don't worry."

I could tell by her face and the way she said "don't worry" that she was worried.

She must've seen something in my face too. "Are you okay?" She sat down next to me, which was nice because she was in a hurry.

"I'm worried about Dad, but also, Sophie's being a pain right when I really need her. I'm not sure if we're even best friends anymore. I think she wants to hang out with Evelyn more than me."

Mom put her arm around me again. "I'm sorry, hon. You and Sophie are growing up. You'll always have each other, but she's going to find other friends with similar interests and so will you. Like the poem says, you should make new friends but—"

"Seriously?" I put my face in my hands.

"Keep the old!" Addie shouted, finishing the poem.

I looked out at Mom between my fingers. "That's your best life advice?"

"Yes," Mom said, smiling. "It's great advice. It was true in kindergarten and still true in middle school."

"I make new friends all the time," Addie said, "but my best friend is Cole."

"That's great, Addie."

"Is Daddy gonna make new friends in jail?"

"Daddy is not going to jail." Mom put her hand on Addie's shoulder. "It's a big misunderstanding. No one thinks Daddy would do anything wrong." She turned toward me. "Can I talk to you privately a minute?"

I followed her out of the kitchen and down the hall. She stopped in front of the fireplace in the living room. "Someone from town sent those death threats," she whispered. "They're still out there. Don't open the door to any strangers. If you go into town, take the road, not the greenway trail. Be aware of your surroundings and be home by dark."

"Mom." It took all my willpower to keep from rolling my eyes. "No one's threatening us. We'll be fine."

"Still, promise me you'll do as I ask."

"I promise."

"Okay." She glanced at her watch. "I better get going, or I'll be late." She one-armed hugged me again. "I'm sorry you and Sophie aren't getting along. We can talk more tonight."

"Okay."

"Addie, be good and listen to Emma!" she yelled over her shoulder as she headed to the door. "Love you, girls."

Addie ran into the living room. "Bye, Mommy!" She turned to me as the front door closed. "What should we do first?"

"Eat." I had to make a plan. If I was going to search Mr. Zauber's farm with Jeb, I had to figure out what to do with Addie. Maybe she could hang out with Cole at the creamery.

Addie skipped back to the kitchen and hopped onto a counter stool. I grabbed a Smoky Mountain Vanilla Haze cream soda from the fridge and plopped down next to her with my cinnamon roll. Cody sat at my feet, looking at my roll longingly and wagging his tail. Before I could take a bite, the doorbell rang, sending him into a barking frenzy.

"I'll get it," I said, sliding off the stool and maneuvering around Cody. "Stay here."

"You're not 'posed to open the door to strangers."

"Were you eavesdropping? I'm not. I'm gonna see who it is first."

It was Sophie. She held a jar with a butterfly chrysalis taped to the top in her hands. "I found it on the ground," she said. "I don't think it's hurt." She held it out to me. "It's for you. I'm sorry for being in such a bad mood this morning."

"It's okay." I moved out of the doorway so she could come in. Taking the jar, I held it up to the light. The chrysalis was lime green with a gold-and-black band around the top. Soon, I'd be able to see the wings of the butterfly smooshed up inside. It was a great present.

Addie bopped up next to me, craning her neck to get a better look. I knelt so she could see better. "Did you know the caterpillar turns to liquid inside here and then completely reforms as a butterfly? It's called the pupa stage."

"Gross! How long till it's a butterfly?"

"Like, ten days-ish."

"That's so cool. I want one."

"If another one falls, you can have it," Sophie said. "You guys wanna go to the butterfly garden? There're more chrysalises there. You can see the butterfly through some. They may emerge soon."

"We're not supposed to go on the greenway trail," Addie said.

"It's okay. Mr. and Mrs. Zauber and a bunch of the Garden Club and Monarch Project people are around." Sophie squatted down and rubbed the side of Cody's head.

"Mom said no." Addie put her hands on her hips.

"She also said I was in charge and to listen to me. We'll take the road part of the way—past the Zaubers'—and then cut over close to the butterfly garden. Mom won't care since adults are around."

Addie shook her head.

"We can hang out there for a bit, and then we'll go to the creamery, get some ice cream, and see if Cole can play. We'll ride back home with Dad."

"That's a great plan," Sophie said.

Addie smiled. "Okay. Can I get Blue Ridge Blueberry?"

"Sure."

Sophie was right. It was a great plan, but I had something else in mind. Jeb could meet us, and we could investigate the Zaubers' on the way. Mr. and Mrs. Zauber would probably be at the butterfly garden for a while, so the coast was clear. I'd get Sophie to watch Addie and keep her eye out for the Zaubers. She'd text us if she saw anything. It was the perfect plan.

"I'll grab my stuff, and we can go in a minute." I ran up the stairs to my room while Sophie sat on the ground, petting Cody and explaining the life cycle of a monarch to Addie. I was thankful they hadn't followed me.

I plopped down on my bed and sent a text to Jeb. I've got to babysit my sister, but Sophie's here. She'll help. They want to go to the butterfly garden. We can sneak into the Zaubers' on the way. They can keep watch for us.

Jeb: Sophie? Really? She hates me. What makes you think she'll keep watch?

Me: She will. Trust me.

Jeb: K. Everybody is watching the game, so I should be able to climb out the bedroom window. Be there in a sec.

I redid my ponytail and put on some lip balm, pausing to study my reflection. I didn't look like a werewolf hunter at all. I was too little. Someone who hunted werewolves would be tall and muscular and in their twenties, or at least in high school. They'd be mean too and really confident in their werewolf-hunting ability. I was none of those things.

But I did have the silver moonstone necklace. I held it up to the mirror and manifested Mrs. Bearpaw's words. "This stone will help you channel your feminine potential. When you wear this, you'll be reminded that you can do anything." I didn't doubt her, but I went ahead and put on my silver cross earrings to be safe. I figured I should use all the help I could get.

Then, I took the wolfsbane out of my backpack, poured it out on my desk, and smashed it up in little bits. I dumped it into my water bottle and shook it up. After that, I went to Addie's room and found two pink squirt guns in her toy box. I filled them up slowly over the bathroom sink and stuck them in my backpack. Looking into the mirror, I held the moonstone up and repeated Mrs. Bearpaw again. "You are a powerful girl." I gave myself a smile. "Let's do this!"

Now I had to tell Sophie Jeb was coming. She was going to freak.

I took a few deep breaths and went back into the living room. "Jeb just texted me," I said slowly.

Sophie looked up, scowling. "What did he want?"

"He's coming over."

She jumped up, practically knocking Addie off the couch. "Seriously? Didn't someone threaten him? He can't come here. It's not safe."

"Yeah!" Addie jumped up too. "It's not safe. Mom said not to talk to strangers."

Of course, she'd take Sophie's side. "He's not a stranger. He's my friend."

Sophie crossed her arms. "You've known him for about twenty-four hours. How is he your friend?"

Addie crossed her arms too. "Yeah. How?"

Ugh. They were so annoying. "You guys should give him a chance. He's really nice and funny—"

"He. Is. Not!" Sophie yelled. "He's destroying the whole town."

"Yeah!" Addie said. "The whole town!"

"I'm working on that. He was really interested in the butterflies yesterday. If we can show him how the ski resort will mess everything up, maybe he'll change his mind."

Sophie rolled her eyes. "Fat chance. We took him to Paul's Peak, and he couldn't stop talking about ski runs and how he'd do a three-sixty on his snowboard. He's a self-absorbed, bratty, rich kid."

"Yeah," Addie said. "Bratty rich kid!"

The anger simmering inside me was about to explode out. "Addie, quit repeating everything Sophie says! *You're* being the brat. You don't even know what you're talking about."

"Well, she's right. He is." Sophie's anger was simmering too. She paced back and forth in front of the couch.

I took a slow deep breath. I couldn't lash out. I needed their help. "He's not. He's gonna help me clear Dad," I said softly. "We're gonna find out who sent the death threat."

Addie's eyes got really wide. "That's not safe. I'm telling Mom."

"If you do, I'll tell her you and Cole ate all the Girl Scout cookies instead of delivering them."

"Okay, okay!" she said, waving her arms.

The doorbell rang, making Cody bark again. "He's here. You guys can go to the butterfly garden without us if you want."

Sophie moved in front of me and the door, arms crossed. "What are you really up to, Emma? How are you guys gonna find out who sent the death threat?"

"We've got an idea. I could use your help, but you've gotta go along with what I say. You're either in or out. No halfway." I weaved around her and opened the door.

Jeb flashed his smile and walked in. He wore a black baseball hat backward, a black hoodie with black checks up the sleeves, and gray athletic shorts. He had great style. The tension in my body relaxed. When he was around, I felt lighter, happier. Cody liked him too. He ran up and licked his hands. Jeb leaned down and scratched his chin.

"Hi," Addie said, bopping in front of me. "You're really cute."

I had to laugh. She switched from "bratty rich kid" to "really cute" really fast.

The tops of Jeb's ears turned tomato-red. "Thanks. So are you."

Sophie looked annoyed. "What's the plan?"

"We wanna check out the Zaubers' property," I said.

"What for?"

"To see what we can find out. Only a few people knew where Jeb was staying, and one of them was Mr. Zauber."

"Wait." Sophie shot me a defiant glare. "You think Mr. Zauber threatened Jeb's dad? That's crazy. He'd never."

I shrugged. "People are freaked about the ski resort. I don't think Mr. Zauber would hurt anybody, but maybe he'd try to scare them. It's gonna be right next to his farm. You know how private he is."

"Exactly. No one is allowed on their property. You know that." Sophie had her debate face on. The same intense look she'd given during the climate-change speeches at school. "It really tore up Mr. Zauber when those kids drowned. He doesn't want it to happen again."

"We're not going by the river. We're just gonna look around." I shot her intense stare back at her. She wasn't going to out-debate me. Not on this.

"You should leave it to the police. If they want to investigate Mr. Zauber, let them do it." She wasn't breaking eye contact. It was getting uncomfortable, but I wasn't going to be the first one to look away.

"I did tell them," Jeb said. "They've zeroed in on Emma's dad since Zauber had some sort of alibi."

"Then, they've looked into it. You don't need to."

The anger I'd been pushing down rose up and spilled out. "All I need you to do is keep watch!" I yelled. "You and Addie can hang around the Zaubers' driveway. If you see them coming, text us. That's it. But we're gonna go either way—with you or without."

"You can use my board," Jeb said quietly, holding it out in front of him. "It's a Jesse Marxx original."

Sophie turned her glare to Jeb. "I don't wanna use your stupid skateboard!"

"I do! Can I?" Addie said, jumping up and down. "This's fun. We're like spies. Sometimes, Cole and I spy on his mom and dad when they're making ice cream. I know everything that's in their secret recipe."

Sophie stood, glaring with her hands on her hips. After a minute, she let out a loud, dramatic sigh. "Fine. I don't think Mr. Zauber had anything to do with it, but if it'll make you feel better, then check it out. Addie and I will skateboard on the road, and I'll text you if I see anything."

I ran to her and gave her a hug. "You're awesome. The best friend ever."

She kept her hands on her hips and didn't hug me back.

I got my board from the garage, and we headed out. The sun was low in the sky. We didn't have much longer until it got dark. Jeb and I skated down the road to the Zaubers' while Sophie and Addie walked behind us.

Jeb couldn't resist doing a few tricks down the hill. He blew ahead of me and jumped up high in an ollie, landed, flipped the board around in a kickflip, landed, and gained speed. He jumped up again like a regular kickflip—spinning the board three-sixty, but his body turned in the air too, so he was facing me. He met my eyes and grinned as his board hit the road. Then, he spun himself and the board back the other way and kept on skating.

We rolled to a stop in front of the Zaubers' driveway. Rows and rows of pines guarded his farm behind a high fence. The driveway curved into the trees, hiding whatever lay at the end.

Jeb pulled his silver chain out from under his shirt. "You scared?"

"Not really," I lied, running the moonstone back and forth on the chain, trying to channel my feminine strength.

Addie and Sophie caught up, stood next to us, and peered down the driveway too.

Jeb flipped his board up with his foot, caught it in his hand, and leaned it toward Addie. "This is a big deal. No one ever borrows my board."

She broke out into a huge grin and took it from his hand.

"What are you even looking for?" Sophie asked.

"Clues." I handed her my board. "You ready?" I turned toward Jeb.

"Let's roll," he said.

We raced across the road to the Zaubers' farm. Sunlight flickered through the trees. Shadows of their wide branches seemed to reach for us. I ignored the creepy feeling, ducked under the gate, and raced down the narrow driveway.

We turned the corner and slowed down, stopping next to the trees. I took the squirt guns out of my backpack. "Wolfsbane water," I said, handing one to Jeb.

He squirted me in the neck.

"Geez!" I yelled. "That's cold! We're supposed to squirt the werewolf, not each other."

"You said it'd repel him, right? Like, keep him away? We should drench ourselves."

"Not yet." I wiped my neck with my hand. "We want to find him, take a picture, and then get away. We'll squirt him and ourselves then."

"Oh, right." He stuck the squirt gun in his back pocket.

"Okay. Let's figure out where we are." I took my phone and pulled up the map.

"I know where we are. We're in the middle of the Zaubers' driveway."

I ignored him and clicked on our location. An aerial view showed the driveway curved through the trees several yards, then went through a clearing and stopped at a house to the north. Across the field on the west side of the farm, there was another building close to the woods. "Let's check out this one," I said, zooming in on the building.

We snuck along the edge of the woods, moving slowly so we wouldn't get scratched by branches blocking our path. A lone crow perched on a branch near the building. It cocked its head sideways, watching us as we inched closer.

The building was an old barn. It looked like no one had used it in years. The red roof was a faded orange color and damaged with a bunch of holes. The brown wood sides ranged from completely faded white to deep gray. Some of the wood planks were missing, and there was a big dark hole in the side. A black sign hung sideways. *BEWARE OF DOG*, it yelled in faded red letters. Tall grass grew up around the barn, but the grass on the road to the barn was smashed down, like somebody still went in and out. The forest began almost right behind the barn, with the ground sloping upward where the mountain started.

"If a clown comes outta that barn, I'm running," Jeb said.

"Shut up." My heart sped up, but I laughed and gently punched him in the arm.

We dashed the few yards across the clearing and stopped at the hole in the wall. Inside the barn, hay was scattered around, with some tied up in barrels. The evening sun shined through the holes, splashing light between dark shadows.

Floorboards creaked and popped as we climbed inside. Dust and hay flew up around us, making the air stale and musty. Part of the barn was behind a wall of rotting two-by-fours. It was next to a half-wall and a falling wood plank fence where animals must have lived in the past. Above that area, there was a hayloft with a rickety ladder. An old wagon covered in dust sat toward the back of the barn next to three wagon wheels. There were two ten-feet-long rusty saws with a handle on each end, and several old items I couldn't identify hanging on the walls. Hanging in the middle, there was a yoke I recognized from my history class. It was used with bulls to plow a field. Everything looked ancient.

A tingling sensation ran from the roots of my hair down to my toes. It was the same eerie feeling I'd had when I saw the ghost looking out the Coopers' barn window. "It seems really creepy in here," I whispered.

"Yeah."

"Let's see what's behind the wall."

We huddled together and walked slowly. His fingers brushed mine, and he grabbed my hand. My stomach flipped around and around. I couldn't tell if I was scared of the barn or excited that Jeb was holding my hand. My brain swirled.

We rounded the corner and stopped quickly—a werewolf!

Jeb yelled in surprise, squeezing my hand. I shook him off and pulled out my squirt gun and shot a long stream of water. My heart beat loud and hard, like it was going to explode out of my chest.

But it wasn't real. Leaning against the barn wall was a huge oil painting of a man turning into a wolf. He looked at lot like Mr. Zauber but way younger, like in his twenties. He wore old-fashioned clothes—maybe from the 1800s—like the guy from the *Little Women* movie. He had on a light-brown vest under a dark-brown suitcoat. A red scarf was tucked into the vest. The painting was in panels, so the first panel was only the guy, and in the next, fur popped out of his ripping clothes, and his teeth grew larger. Then, his whole body became thicker, and his clothes ripped almost off Incredible Hulk-like, but he wasn't green. He was covered in reddish fur. He looked like he was screaming in pain. In the last picture, he'd turned into a huge wolf and didn't resemble a person at all. His amber eyes stared right at us. His yellow fangs were several inches long, and his mouth was open, like he was getting ready to take a huge bite out of us. Whoever painted it was wicked talented.

Jeb laughed nervously. "Dude, that scared me. It looks so real."

"Me too. Do you think it's the Toggle Road Beast?" I stuck my squirt gun back into my pocket and pulled out my phone to take a picture. I couldn't get over how much the guy looked like Mr. Zauber, but it couldn't be. He was old but not *that* old.

Suddenly, a panicked scream cut through the air.

Jeb and I ran to the front of the barn. Sophie was yelling my name and running toward the barn, pulling Addie by the hand behind her. One of Addie's pigtails had come undone and flew around wildly. A gigantic dog raced around the corner behind them.

Wait ... not a dog.

A wolf. Like the one in the painting. The Toggle Road Beast.

My body froze.

"Let's go up!" Jeb dashed toward the ladder. "It won't be able to get up there."

I wasn't so sure, but there was no time to argue. There was no way out. I sprinted to Addie, grabbed her, and put her on the ladder. She scurried up behind Jeb, then Sophie, and then me. The ladder shook and creaked like it was going to crack in half. The wolf ran into the barn, put his front legs on the ladder, and growled and snapped within inches of my foot. He was reddish-gray with beady amber eyes, pointed ears, and huge yellow teeth, exactly like the painting. He snapped and snapped, but Jeb was right. He couldn't climb up to the hayloft.

I took Addie's hand and stepped carefully around the holes. The floor moaned and groaned, as if our weight was too much to hold. I pictured us crashing through, landing on the ground, and being mauled by the wolf who snarled below us.

Addie squeezed my hand and stopped walking. Her whole body shook. I put my arm around her and pulled her to my side.

Jeb stood still, his arms slightly out to his sides like he was skateboarding. Sophie leaned over and put her hands on her knees. Her eyes were wide, and each breath came out a high-pitched wheeze.

"Are you okay?" I asked.

She glared at me. I could feel anger and fear shooting out of her eyes. "*None* of us are okay."

I quickly scanned the hayloft. I had to get us out of this quick. "Let's jump out the back window. We'll get a good head start because it'll take him a minute to figure out where we are. We can run through the woods and climb over the fence to the road."

"I think we should wait," said Sophie in between wheezes. "He'll leave eventually. He can't climb. If we stay up here, we'll be safe."

Addie leaned closer to me. "I'm scared. I don't wanna walk across the floor. I don't wanna stand here, and I don't wanna jump."

The wolf ran back and forth by the ladder. His lips curled around his teeth, and his growl was low and deep.

"You'll be fine, Addie," Jeb said. "Trust me. I'll go first." He walked slowly, pausing after each step. The floor clicked and popped. He stopped at the edge of the window. "It's not far. You can do it. Hang down, and I'll catch you."

I squeezed Addie's hand. "We'll go slow." She nodded.

We inched across the floor, trying to avoid holes but slipping and sliding on hay.

Sophie stayed put. "This is a bad idea." Her eyes were squeezed shut, and she was breathing fast.

The wolf snarled up at us through the hole in the floor as he paced back and forth. His amber eyes flashed angrily, just like Mr. Zauber's had when he told us to stay off the Coopers' property. *Mr. Zauber?* It couldn't be. Could it?

"Don't look down," I whispered to Addie. We kept inching forward. Stopping next to Jeb, we looked over the edge. He was right. It wasn't far.

"Easy," Jeb said, and he leaped out the window, landing with a thud and rolling to the ground. He sprung up on his feet. "See?"

"You can do it." I let go of Addie's hand and helped her climb out. She hung for a second and let go with a loud grunt. Jeb caught her and slid her softly to the ground.

The wolf stopped pacing and sniffed the air below the window.

I turned back to Sophie. "Walk toward me. I'll help you."

She shook her head. "I can't. I'm too scared." Her eyes were still squeezed tight.

"Sophie, open your eyes and keep them on me. Don't look down. You can do this. Breathe slow and steady."

She opened her eyes slowly and shuffled toward me. The floorboards shook. A long crack popped open between us. Chunks of floor showered the wolf. He snarled and jumped up toward the hole. Sophie froze.

I gripped the side of the window to steady myself. The moonstone necklace thumped against me. I grabbed it and reflected the setting orange sun into the wolf's eyes. He winced. Then, I shot him with the wolfsbane water, hitting him right in the middle of his eyes.

He shook the water off his head and growled.

I quickly reached over the hole and grabbed Sophie's hand. "Open your eyes, Sophie. You have to jump!"

She nodded, but I wasn't sure if she could do it. She was breathing so fast.

"Jump on three. One ... two ... three!"

The floor cracked again, filling the air between us with dust. Sophie leaped over the hole, and I pulled her with me out the window. The ground rushed toward me in a hazy blur. I landed with a jolt, fell, and rolled out of Sophie's way. I hopped up and put Addie on my back so she could ride piggyback.

The wolf yelped loudly as bits of the floor collapsed down on top of him.

We sprinted through the maze of trees, ducking under branches and jumping over roots. My feet beat out a frantic rhythm as sharp twigs grabbed my clothes and scraped my face and arms. My lungs felt like they were going to burst. The sun was getting lower, and I couldn't see well.

We finally reached the fence that surrounded Mr. Zauber's property. Jeb climbed over quickly, and the three of us helped Addie. Sophie and I scurried over at the same time. We ran several more yards, collapsed in the grass, and tried to catch our breath.

I was in shock. Mr. Zauber wasn't hiding the wolf. He was the wolf. Jeb was right. "We proved it," I said when I could finally breathe. "The Toggle Road Beast is back. It's a wolf-shifter, not a werewolf, right? Hopefully not a werewolf."

"Oh, c'mon." Sophie shot up. "You've lost your mind. What we proved is that there are red wolves in Black Mountain. Do you think it's hurt?"

Sophie was stubborn, but this was too much, even for her. "Did you actually see it? Red wolves aren't that big."

"I sort of saw it. Enough to know it was like the red wolves we looked up."

"No, it was huge. That wolf was man-sized, like the wolves in the books from Erin's store," I said.

"There's no other explanation, Emma. You were just scared," Sophie said. "Your brain was playing tricks on you."

"My brain was not playing tricks on me. My brain knows the difference between a red wolf and a ... whatever that was. Your eyes were closed most of the time. Did you even look at it?"

"We'll email the EPA." Sophie went on like I hadn't even said anything. "They'll stop the ski resort since red wolves are going extinct."

Jeb jumped up. "Hold up. We're not stopping anything, and I agree with Emma. That was no regular wolf. Did you see its fangs? And how fast it ran?"

Jeb was right. Sophie's brain was playing tricks, not ours. She was choosing what she wanted to see and believe.

Addie sat up and hugged herself. "I don't know what that was, but it was super scary. I think we should get out of here. What if it jumps the fence?"

Sophie hopped up off the ground. "We have to go back with a camera. One with a good night lens."

Addie looked like she was going to cry. "No! Let's go home, Emma, please."

I stood and offered her my hand. "You wanna ride piggyback?" I asked.

She nodded.

"Hey, kiddo," Jeb said. "Can I take a turn? Your sis is probably beat."

Addie nodded again, and Jeb bent down so she could get on his back. She climbed up and wrapped her arms around him. She didn't look scared anymore. Kind of happy, actually. I smiled.

"Where's my board?" Jeb asked.

"We left them in the bushes by the road. Across from the driveway," Sophie said.

"I don't wanna go back there." I looked at Jeb. "Let's get the boards tomorrow when it's daylight."

"Coolio," he said. "Probably easier to find them in the daylight anyway."

The trees blew back and forth against the violet sky as we made our way back to my house. They looked like giants with clawed arms. I shivered and rubbed my arms.

"You cold?" Jeb put Addie down and peeled off his hoodie. "Put this on."

I took his hoodie and pulled it on, breathing in as it went over my face. It smelled like minty shampoo and a little musty but in a good way. It felt like a warm hug.

He looped a finger through the hair tie on my wrist. "I'll trade you."

I nodded, so he slipped it off my wrist and twisted it around his.

Addie hopped up on his back again, and we continued walking quickly through the flickering shadows.

A wolf howled in the distance.

Chapter 10

Repetition: repeating the same or similar elements throughout the design

I woke up with the sun streaming in through the cracks of my blinds. Memories of a wild dream about a huge wolf on the Zaubers' farm flashed in my head. But it hadn't been a dream. The fact that I was still wearing Jeb's hoodie proved it. I pulled the collar up to my nose and breathed in, replaying the scene in my head—him pulling it off and handing it to me and then sliding my hair tie off my wrist.

Addie lay curled up next to me, snoring softly. She'd slipped in during the night after having a nightmare. I knew how she felt. My body was still tense and on high alert.

I stared at the ceiling, replaying the whole strange wolf encounter in my mind. There was nothing about it that made any sense. I'd been around Mr. Zauber my whole life. He was a kind and gentle old man, not the kind of guy you'd expect to turn into a beast and threaten to kill someone. He loved flowers and wanted everyone to love them too. He planted them around town, the greenway, and at Camp Eagle Crest. He led workshops in town about organic gardening. He always smiled and said hello whenever he saw me. When the Environmental Club worked in the butterfly garden, he'd take the time to teach us about what we were planting and ask us about school. He never talked down to us like we were just kids.

He'd been in my house hundreds of times. When Mom had asked him and Mrs. Zauber about helping with the Monarch Project a few years ago, they jumped at the idea. Mrs. Zauber always brought a pie over, and then, they'd spend hours around our kitchen table, planning and talking. Mr. and Mrs. Zauber became experts on monarchs.

But just because he loved flowers, gardening, and butterflies didn't mean he couldn't be the Toggle Road Beast. Right? Maybe the beast was a wolf-shifter like Mrs. Bearpaw had said. Maybe it was a protector—not of people but of the land Jeb wanted to destroy.

Whatever he was, Mr. Zauber was definitely trying to hide behind that fortress of bushes and trees. If we got a picture, like Sophie wanted to, we might be able to use it to convince him to admit he left the death threat. Dad could go to jail. I needed to get Mr. Zauber to confess.

Addie rolled over, stretched, yawned, and sat up. She turned toward me, eyes wide. "We gotta tell Mommy and Daddy."

I sat up and put my hands on her shoulders. "We can't, not yet. We will, but it's not the right time. They've got so much they're already worried about. We can't give them anything else."

"But we're not safe. What if it gets us?"

"It won't. It's a wild animal. It chased us because we were on its property."

"You think it lives with Mr. Zauber?"

I thought it *was* Mr. Zauber, but I wasn't going to say that. "Maybe he's been hiding it. That's why he has all the signs and fences."

"Do you think it can jump the fence?"

Yes, but I wasn't going to say that either.

Addie read my face though. "What if it comes into our yard? What about Cody? What if it gets him?"

"I don't think it'll come into the yard."

Addie fell back on the bed. "What do you mean you 'don't *think* it will'? Ahhh! We're all gonna die!" She threw her arm over her face, covering her eyes with her elbow. "All I can see are its big wet fangs and weird yellow eyes!"

"Shhh! Listen to me. Think about the beast in *Beauty and the Beast*. Remember how all the townspeople wanted to kill him because he looked scary? He was only a threat when they stormed his castle."

"This is real life."

"All I'm saying is we should be careful but not panic. We need to stay away from the Zaubers' property. How did it start chasing you anyway?"

Addie got still. She kept her eyes covered with her elbow. "I don't know." Her voice cracked.

"You've gotta tell me everything, Addie."

"I wasn't good at skateboarding. It was boring, and I wanted to go with you."

"And?"

"I put Jeb's Jesse Marxx original in the bushes and climbed under the driveway gate. Sophie was mad. She told me to stay with her."

I sighed. "You kept going."

"Uh-huh, but I didn't know where you were. So, I was looking around. Sophie yelled for me to come back. That's when I saw it."

"Addie!" I moved her arm off her face and looked her in the eye. "You're a hero. If you hadn't come around the corner and warned us, we never would've have seen it." I pulled her up and gave her a hug.

Her eyes filled with tears. "What would've it had done if we hadn't gotten away?"

"I don't know." And I didn't want to find out. I grabbed my phone and hopped out of bed. "Remember, we can't tell anyone. Not yet."

"Okay."

"Pinky promise."

Addie held her hand out, and we wrapped our pinkies together. "I swear, I won't tell," she said.

"If Addie tells, her rock collection will turn to dust," I said in the creepiest voice I could make. I squeezed her pinky with mine.

The fear left her face as she laughed and threw my pillow at me. "You're not a witch. You can't curse me."

"How do you know?" I said in the creepy voice. Laughing, I threw the pillow back at her.

She kept laughing and tossed the pillow back at me. It was a relief to see her relax. It'd been a huge mistake to take her. I thought they'd be safe in the road. It never crossed my mind Addie would follow us. I put all of us in danger. But if she and Sophie hadn't been there ... I didn't even want to think about what would've happened to me and Jeb.

Now that she wasn't scared and I was sure she wasn't going to tell, my work was done. I whacked her with the pillow. "Now get out of my room. I've got stuff to do."

"Like text Jeb?" She giggled and hugged the pillow. "He's *so* cute!"

I could feel the redness on my face as I tried not to smile. "Get out."

"Is he your boyfriend now?"

"Addie—"

"He *gave* you his hoodie! He *gave* you his hoodie!" she sang as she jumped up and down on my bed.

"We're only friends. Now get out!" I grabbed the pillow and threw at her again. I felt light and giggly, like her.

She jumped off the bed and skipped to the door. "Emma's got a boyfriend! Emma's got a boyfriend!" she sang.

"No, I don't!" Giggling, I closed the door behind her and leaned back against it. I fanned my hot face with my hands, took a deep breath, and blew it out.

I checked my phone. I had over one hundred notifications from Instagram ... and they were all from Jeb. He'd liked all my posts, even the awkward little kid ones. Yikes. He commented on one of me at the beach with huge purple sunglasses and a red floppy beach hat. I looked like one of those goofy grandmas from the greeting cards Dad sold in the store. Hi, he'd typed. Just scrolling down on your page to say hello and nice lid.

Oh, God. Why hadn't I deleted that picture?

But even though I was embarrassed, my face was stuck in a huge smile. Bahaha u did nottt, I typed under his comment.

He'd also texted me. That was insane. You want to hang later and discuss? I can go out, but I got to bring Tweedledum with me. He wants to run on the greenway, so he'll give us space.

Me: Sounds good. I'd added an exclamation point but backspaced over it.

Jeb: They don't know your dad's the locksmith though. So don't say anything.

Me: Great.

Jeb: Can you get my board and meet there at 11:00?

Me: Coolio.

Jeb: Haha hey, that's my line!

I also had a text from Sophie. I can't believe we saw a RED WOLF!!!!!

I guess Sophie didn't have the same nightmare that I did. She was still totally delusional about what we'd seen. It was crazy. Jeb and I thought Mr. Zauber was the Toggle Road Beast, but Sophie was the one with her head in the clouds.

Me: That wasn't a red wolf.

Sophie: We've got to get back and get a pic. Then you'll see. Maybe after we're done in the garden?

Dang it. I forgot Sophie and I were supposed to work in the garden. I'd just have to take Jeb with me. It'd give me another chance to convince him not to build his resort ... if the Toggle Road Beast hadn't already scared him away.

Me: Great idea! Jeb wants to hang. I want him to see the butterfly garden, so I'm bringing him. Then we can figure it out. Sound good?

Three little dots popped up under my message, so I knew she was responding, but then they disappeared, and there was a long pause. Then three dots, then a pause, then three dots. I could feel her anger before she even responded.

Sophie: You're wasting your time. We've got what we need. Once the EPA sees there's RED WOLVES in the woods, they'll never let them build there.

Sophie was right about the picture being convincing, but it would convince her, not me or the EPA. Once she saw it—*really* saw it—there'd be no denying the truth.

Me: We should cover all our angles as a backup.

Sophie: He's a hopeless case.

Me: So you've said. Can you meet in front of the Zaubers' in an hour and show me where you ditched the skateboards?

Long pause again and then: Sure.

I texted Cami next. Are you free today? I got to talk to you about the Toggle Road Beast.

Cami: Did you see something again?

Me: Yes, but I need to tell you in person.

Cami: I'm pet-sitting for Alma while Tiá Lupé works in the Butterfly Garden. I'm going to run with her down the greenway. Meet me there?

I ran downstairs, quickly heated up a cinnamon roll, grabbed a vanilla cream soda from the fridge, and ran back upstairs. My life felt tangled up, like a fly caught in a spider's web. Dad was a suspect for threatening Chester, who wanted to destroy the mountain that was inhabited by a monster and was the father of the guy I was crushing on, whom my best friend hated. Totally insane. But the wolf was the key to everything. There was no way Jeb would want his dad to buy the property now, and if I could prove the wolf was Mr. Zauber, he'd admit to threatening Jeb's dad.

I sat my breakfast down on my desk and pulled out the paper Mrs. Bearpaw had given me. It told the story of two huge red dogs wrestling and swimming on the banks of the Swannanoa River. The legend said they lived in an underwater cave. It didn't mention werewolves or wolf-shifters, but what else could they be? Mr. Zauber was really old, and his grandfather lived here before him, so maybe there's been generations of wolf people in his family.

I flipped open *The Beast of Toggle Road*. It began with a sighting by a guy named Lude A. Chris, whose car broke down on the side of the road.

> *The Beast stood on its hind legs far above Lude's car. In the moonlight, Lude could see every detail. Mud dangled on the beast's matted fur. Foam dripped from its lips, curling over long fangs. Razor-sharp claws extended from huge, dark paws. Amber eyes pierced straight into Lude's soul. The Beast swiped at the car.*

Whoa. A chill went through me, and I slammed the book closed. The wolf in the barn had looked exactly like that. I stuffed the books back into my bag so Jeb and I could look at them later. We needed to do research before we went back.

I chugged my cream soda and finished the roll. Then, I went to my closet, trying to figure out what to wear. I went with black leggings, a long T-shirt with geometric red and black designs appliqued on the front, and my white tennis shoes I'd decorated with a black Sharpie. I usually didn't wear them to skate because I didn't want to tear them up. Today, I didn't care. I braided my hair, slipped the moonstone necklace on, and then sent Sophie a text to see if she was ready.

The skateboards were in the bushes right at the edge of the Zaubers' driveway. Jeb's Jesse Marxx original looked fine, just a little muddy. Sophie and I grabbed them and ran until we were safely down the street, then I hopped on Jeb's board, and Sophie rode mine. She was in a really good mood. Probably because she thought she'd be able to stop the ski resort with the "red wolf" photo. Whatever the reason, it was nice to have the old Sophie back.

We skated down the road and over to the greenway. The sun hid behind the clouds, but bits of light shined through, making everything look yellow. We stopped at trail marker four.

"I'm meeting Jeb here." I hopped off and flipped his board up like he had, but I missed. It hit my shin.

Sophie laughed. "Nice."

"He makes it look so easy." I laughed too and tried again.

"I can show you." Jeb popped up from around the corner. He had on the green baseball hat and a navy-blue T-shirt. There were dark circles under his eyes, and he looked a little pale.

I rolled his board over to him. He stopped it with his foot, flipped it up, and caught it in his hand. My hair tie was still around his wrist.

"Show-off," I said, laughing.

Sophie smiled, which seemed like a huge breakthrough. She usually scowled at Jeb. Or anytime I said his name. "I'm going to go work in the butterfly garden. You guys coming?" she asked.

"Yeah, in a bit. Can you show me how to do that?" I asked Jeb.

"Sure."

Sophie rolled her eyes and left us alone on the path.

"Where's your bodyguard?"

"Not far. He can probably hear us. Tweedledum?"

"Shut up, kid." A voice came from around the bend. "It's Mr. Dum to you." This was followed by a deep chuckle.

"See? He's chill." Jeb said.

Tweedledum appeared from around the corner. He looked more like a normal person today—huge but normal in athletic pants, T-shirt, and running shoes. "I'm jogging to town. I expect to pass you on my way back. Don't try to lose me."

"'Kay," Jeb said.

Tweedledum set a timer on his watch and ran past us.

"Alone at last," Jeb said.

I wasn't sure if he meant alone with me or *alone* alone, but my stomach flipped around like I was McTwisting at a skate park.

"That was insane last night, huh? I had some wild dreams," he said.

"Me too."

"Didn't sleep much." He glanced around the path as if somebody might've been hiding in the woods.

"Listen to this," I said, dropping my bag. I pulled out *The Beast of Toggle Road* and read him the Lude A. Chris part, stopping in the same place. "It looked exactly like that," I said.

Jeb shuddered. "That had to be it. What happened to that dude, Lude A. Chris?"

"I don't know. I was too freaked out to read any more."

"Keep going."

"It shook the car," I read. "Lude frantically locked the doors and turned the key in the engine. It whirled and sputtered. The Beast swiped again. The car rattled, knocking Lude into the passenger side. The Beast staggered to the other side and crashed its paw through the window, knocking glass across the inside of the car. Lude flipped to the back as—"

"Okay, okay, that's enough." Jeb took off his hat and wiped his forehead. "Geez."

Fear prickles started at the top of my head and shot all the way to my toes. I closed the book and stuck it back in my bag. "He must've got away if he told his story," I said.

"Like us." Jeb flipped his hat back on.

I nodded. "Sophie and I are gonna go back tonight. We're gonna get a picture."

"You're crazy." Jeb took his hat back off and flipped it around nervously. "But it's gotta be done."

I nodded. "After we get one, we'll show it to Mr. Zauber and get him to confess to the death threat."

Jeb's eyes went wide. "You're gonna blackmail him?"

I hadn't thought about it like that, but I guess that was what I'd be doing. "He did it. He needs to confess. It's the only way to clear my dad."

"Then he'll leave. He'll leave town, right?" he asked, his voice urgent.

"I don't know if he will."

Jeb's lips went tight.

"You can't build a resort there." My voice cracked.

He wouldn't look me in the eye. "It's Dad, not me."

"If you told him no, would he change his mind?"

Jeb shrugged. "He keeps talking about 'getting back to his roots.' He wants to spend more time here and get out of LA."

Sadness spilled through my whole body. "Even if you don't care about the environment—"

"I do!" He looked up, meeting my eyes. "I'll get Dad to donate money. You can build a bigger and better garden someplace—"

"There's no other place. But besides that, Jeb, there's the Toggle Road Beast. Maybe it's been there for generations." I pulled the sheet Mrs. Bearpaw had given me out of my backpack. "The Cherokee called the land by the Zaubers' and Coopers' property 'where the dogs live.' Maybe it's a wolf-shifter—a protector of the land. It's not gonna leave."

He flipped his hat back on and took the sheet from me. As he read, all the color faded from his face. "I'll go with you tonight," he said, handing the sheet back to me.

"Fine, but Sophie's not into our Toggle Road Beast theory, so we can't bring it up around her."

"I figured." He hopped on his board and tick-tacked around me. "I dig the shoes. You paint those?"

I nodded. He was changing the subject. I knew it, but even so, I felt the redness starting on my neck and rising through my face. I really wished I could control my emotions. I packed up my backpack and flipped it onto my back.

"How's your ollie?" he asked.

"Let me see your board, and I'll let you know."

He stopped his board, laughing. "You're getting cocky now."

He rolled the board to me, and I stopped it with my foot. I pushed off slow, gained a little speed, popped up, levitated perfectly in the air, and landed it. My mood lifted with the board. I wasn't giving up, not yet. I could still make him care—*really* care—about the environment. The garden would change his mind, even if the Toggle Road Beast hadn't. I coasted down the hill, then turned back around toward him, smiling.

"Whoo-hoo!" he cheered, throwing his arms up in the air.

I hopped off his board and bowed.

He ran up to me like he was going to hug me, but instead, he threw his hand up to give me a high five. "That was dope. You got some serious air!"

"Let's ride down to the butterfly garden. There's something I wanna show you."

We jumped on our own boards and skated down the hill. He did a couple ollies, blew by me, and circled back. "I'm teaching you the heelflip next!" He pushed off, gained some speed, and flipped the board in a three-sixty but in the opposite direction of a kickflip.

"Nice!" I yelled.

Tweedledum jogged toward us and nodded hello.

"We're gonna go to the butterfly garden on up the greenway." Jeb yelled.

He gave us a thumbs-up as he passed by.

Chapter 11

Gradation: combining elements by using a series of gradual changes in those elements (for example, small becomes large)

We flew around the corner, and the monarch garden came into view, first at a blurry distance and then shaper and clearer the closer we got. The purples, reds, yellows, and greens looked dull without the depth of shadows the sunlight usually made. I knew every inch of the garden. Not only because I'd helped plant the flowers but also because Ms. Hartford taught her art class outside. Every Saturday, I sat for hours, studying and painting the petals of purple coneflowers, the stems of the oxeye daisies, and mixing the right paint to get the not-quite-blue-or-purple color of the bluets.

The day's grayness did not dull the enthusiasm of the Garden Club. They flitted around like butterflies, pulling weeds, counting eggs, and pruning dead flowers.

Mr. Zauber stopped working when he saw us. He held the big gardening shears halfway open in mid-chop. A large bandage was on the corner of his temple and disappeared under his gardening hat. "Hello, Emma." He stared at the moonstone dangling around my neck.

"Are you okay, Mr. Zauber? What happened to your head?"

"Oh, I took a little fall in the old barn. Something got into the hayloft last night and part of the floor came down. I slipped this morning on some bits of debris." He put his hand up to his head and gently touched his temple. "It's a bit sore, but I'll be fine."

I avoided Jeb's eyes. I knew what he was thinking because I was thinking the same thing. Mr. Zauber must've gotten the cut when the floor fell on him last night. He was definitely the Toggle Road Beast.

I forced a smile. "Well, I'm glad it's not serious. Have you seen any chrysalises? I wanna show Jeb."

Mr. Zauber eyed Jeb up and down with a look of disdain on his face. "There's some on the milkweed behind the coneflowers." He gestured with his thumb. "Make sure your friend knows proper butterfly etiquette."

Jeb followed me off the greenway trail and down the little path between the flowers. "Yeah, he slipped in the barn all right," he whispered.

I turned around and nodded slowly. "Exactly. Now I'm positive it was him." I glanced back at Mr. Zauber. "He's watching us," I whispered.

"Great," Jeb whispered back. "I guess we're safe here with all these people around."

I nodded and said loudly, "Keep following me, Jeb. There's something I want you to see."

It wasn't an act. I really did want to show Jeb the butterfly garden. I knew it was a stretch to have him love it as much as I did, but I really wanted him to at least appreciate it—both the beauty and the importance, so he wouldn't destroy it.

"Umm ... there's nothing like poison ivy or anything in here, is there?" Jeb glanced around our feet.

"No."

"Snakes?"

"Maybe, but I've never seen a copperhead or anything. Only rat snakes and garter."

Jeb stopped walking.

"Those won't hurt you. Come on."

He followed slowly with his head down, scanning the ground.

We stopped by the milkweed. There were a few caterpillars on it, crawling around and munching on the leaves. A couple had attached themselves down under leaves and were curled up. I motioned for Jeb to sit down. "These two made a silk pad and attached themselves to the milkweed."

He searched the ground for snakes and bugs and then squatted down next to me. I really wished he wouldn't be so scared of nature. "What's a silk pad?" he asked.

"It holds the caterpillar in place. He's gonna transform soon into a pupa. It's also called a chrysalis."

"How do they ... wait ... what?"

A green blob appeared on the caterpillar's back behind his head. It grew larger and larger as the caterpillar wiggled like an accordion. It looked like it was sucking him up, but really, it was more like he was hanging upside down and pulling on a hoodie. He wiggled faster and faster, shaking and twisting as the green traveled all the way up his body until there was nothing left resembling the caterpillar. A little wad of black skin bunched up at the tip. When the green reached the top, the chrysalis spun and shook. It looked like it spit the balled-up skin to the ground. It just fell though.

Jeb stared in horror. "Gross! Was that the head?"

"It was the skin."

"Oh, okay. Then that was pretty dope. It looked like *Invasion of the Body Snatchers*." Now that he was over the shock, he actually seemed impressed.

"It kind of was, I guess."

The chrysalis continued to wiggle, shake, and shrink. It was bright green with lime stripes, but it slowly turned into a solid green shell. A gold band appeared around the top.

"I thought it spun some kind of silk web. I didn't know the green stuff swallowed it like that."

"It shreds its skin. Then it basically eats itself inside and turns to goo."

"Gross. Then what?"

"It reforms as a butterfly. But the coolest part is the butterfly remembers its life as a caterpillar. They've done research that shows it'll avoid the same smells they taught the caterpillar to avoid."

"And they remember how to get to Mexico by their DNA," Jeb added.

"That's just my theory." I kept my cool, but inside, I was beaming. He remembered! My plan seemed to be working.

"Let's find another caterpillar. I wanna put it on my story." He pulled his phone out of his back pocket and crawled around, searching under the leaves. Evidently, he'd forgotten about his fear of bugs and snakes.

Alma, the hyper Australian shepherd, bounced up to us, pulling Cami along. Alma jumped on Jeb, knocking him facedown into a bee balm bush.

"Get off!" He pushed her away and tried to stand, but Alma kept jumping. "Down, dog! Down!"

"She only speaks Spanish, Jeb," Cami said, gripping the metal ring on Alma's harness. "She doesn't know what you're saying."

"What?"

"Bajate. Bajate!" Cami put her hand on Alma's head and the dog stopped jumping. "Siéntate." Alma sat and wagged her tail. "See?" Cami reached into her bag and pulled out a treat. "She's a good dog."

Jeb and I pet Alma behind her soft velvety ears. "How do you say 'good dog' in Spanish?" Jeb asked.

"Buen chica." Cami ran her hand slowly back and forth on the dog's shoulders.

"Buen chica," Jeb repeated, and Alma looked up with her baby-blue eyes and licked his hand. "Hang on to her. I'm on a hunt," he said as he got back down on the ground and searched around the milkweed.

"What are you guys doing?" Sophie asked as she and Evelyn made their way around the bee balm bush toward us.

"Jeb wants to put a caterpillar transformation on his Insta Story," I said.

Sophie looked bright and excited. "That's amazing. I bet you have a huge platform!" For once, she wasn't looking at Jeb like she wished he'd fall off the face of the earth. Her face had a hint of admiration.

Jeb stopped searching under the milkweed and sat back to look at Sophie. "A what?"

"She means followers," Evelyn said.

Sophie was getting revved up now. "You can let them know about the importance of milkweed and how bad insecticides are. Have you ever thought about using your platform to raise awareness?"

"My YouTube channel has skateboarding tutorials."

Sophie didn't roll her eyes. Things were definitely on the upswing. "I'm sure they're great," she said, "but you could post environmental stuff. You could be the Leonardo DiCaprio of our generation."

"Leonardo DiCaprio?"

She shrugged. "He's the first Hollywood guy that came to mind. He's done a lot for the environment."

"He's friends with my dad."

"What? You know Leonardo DiCaprio?" Sophie yelled. A few people looked up from their gardening and stared at us.

Alma jumped on Sophie and barked. Cami grabbed the ring on her harness. "Guarde silencio."

Sophie swooned. "He's met Greta Thunberg. I'm only two degrees away from Greta!"

"What's that mean?" Jeb asked.

Sophie smiled. "Like, I know you, and you know Leo, so I'm one degree away from Leo. Leo knows Greta, so I'm two degrees away from her."

"Right, but who's Greta Thumborg?" Jeb asked.

Sophie's face fell. "Thunberg! Are you serious? She's one of the most influential environmentalists of our time. She was only sixteen when she spoke to the United Nations about climate change."

"Nice. I'll introduce you to Leo once we get our place up and running. He likes to ski too. Then you'll be only one degree away from Greta."

Sophie and Evelyn looked like they wanted to push Jeb off the face of the earth again.

I knew exactly how they felt. My feelings kept bouncing from wanting to hug him to wanting to hurt him. My hopefulness turned to disappointment like the caterpillar morphing into a chrysalis. Hope was the little ball of skin that fell to the ground. Just when I thought I'd made progress.

"You're hopeless." Sophie said what we were all thinking.

"Hopeless and starving. Does your dad have any blueberry pie today?"

She rolled her eyes. "I have no idea."

Jeb stood and brushed the dirt off his shorts. "Let's go get some food. We can walk since you guys don't have boards."

"What makes you think we wanna come?" Sophie asked.

"Yeah." Evelyn nodded and glared at Jeb.

Jeb shrugged.

"Geez, guys." I knocked Sophie gently with my elbow. "Come with us."

"Fine," she said.

"I'm in," Cami said. "Let me find Tiá Lupé and see if she can take her dog back now. We ran two miles on the greenway. Surely, Alma's worn out enough."

"I'll go with you." I needed to fill her in on last night's events … away from Sophie and Evelyn.

Cami tugged gently on the dog's leash. "Vamos, busquemos a tu mamá." The bushes rustled and shook as we walked through. "No, Alma!" Cami yelled as Alma nosed a branch by a monarch. "Don't eat the butterfly! I mean, no comas! No comas! Perro malo!" The dog twisted around, barking like crazy. "Ven!" Cami yelled, pulling the dog away on its leash.

"Hey, Jeb," I said, stopping by the monarch. "Here's a butterfly drying its wings. I think you just missed its transformation."

Jeb ran over to take a video, and I followed Cami and Alma down the path.

As we looked for Cami's aunt, I quietly told her all about our brush with death in the Zaubers' barn.

Her eyes got wider and wider. "Vaya! That sounds like de Cuetlachtli. That's how the wolves are described in the legend."

"We're going back tonight to get a picture. Can you come with us?"

"That's still a hard no, but I'll look at the picture and give you my expert opinion."

We couldn't find Tiá Lupé, but Carlos agreed to watch Alma if Cami brought back some blueberry pie. We followed the loop through the garden and found Sophie and Evelyn singing "Circle of Life" from *The Lion King* as they danced through the white flowers on the hydrangea bushes. Geez. They harmonized perfectly, like they had during the spring choir concert. Somehow, Evelyn managed to bring out fun Sophie. She was always so serious when she was with me. But I couldn't dance or sing. Evelyn was beautiful, graceful, and had an amazing voice.

Cami looked at me and rolled her eyes. "They're probably scaring all the butterflies," she whispered.

I laughed, thankful Cami could come so I wouldn't have to feel so awkward standing there while Sophie and Evelyn looked like they were having the time of their lives.

Jeb popped up behind us with Tweedledum, and we followed the loop the rest of the way to the greenway trail. We didn't see any more caterpillars getting ready to transform, but we did see a couple of chrysalises.

Jeb added them to his story and typed, *Save the monarchs!* I didn't think he was completely serious, but it was still nice. Each little step forward was another move toward him seeing how important the garden and mountain were. Maybe things weren't completely hopeless. He was interested in the monarchs, and he and Sophie had had a conversation without her looking like she wanted to kill him. Well, at least at first. Things I'd thought were impossible were starting to happen. It was a good sign.

As we walked into town, Jeb gave us updates about how many views the post was getting. It was in the hundreds by the time we pulled open the door to Max's Diner. Sophie was pretty excited. I knew what she was thinking. Jeb could be our celebrity tie-in, our own Leonardo DiCaprio.

The inside of the diner smelled like frying fish, barbeque, and pie. The usual lunch crowd chatter made a low hum. Forks scraped and glasses clanged. People crowded into shiny red booths in clusters of those for the resort and those against it. A few tourists sat at the tables scattered through the middle. Some people looked up at Jeb when we walked in, but he didn't seem to notice.

Tweedledum headed to the counter, and Max motioned us over to a booth in the back corner. Sophie sat first, and Evelyn practically pushed us out of the way to sit beside her. Jeb sat across from them. I slid onto the smooth vinyl seat next to him, and Cami hopped in after me, scootching me farther in so my knee bumped Jeb's. My stomach slid back and forth like I was on the ramp at the skate park in Asheville. To distract myself, I studied the daily special board on the other side of the diner, even though I already knew it was Max's Alabama white sauce on pulled pork with roasted chickpeas and fried okra. It was the same every Thursday.

Below the board, the guy we'd seen in the creamery yesterday sat at a two-person table with Willa Cooper. He leaned in close to her with his face red and contorted like he was whisper-yelling. She looked super uncomfortable.

"Who's that with Willa?" I asked Max, nodding toward the guy.

"That's her brother, Paul. Never liked him." Max lowered his voice. "He was a real jerk in high school. Dated Erin. Broke up with her when he started dating someone else in college. He moved out west but came back to town this week when he heard Willa was selling their land."

"What do you think they're fighting about?" I asked.

Max lowered his voice even more and glanced around quickly. "He's against selling but can't do anything 'cause Willa has the most stake in the LLC. Daryl basically left everything to her when Paul moved out west."

"LLC?" I asked.

"Yep. It's a little company Daryl started. He wanted to keep the land as a natural area with hiking trails and rough camping."

"The ski resort is tearing this whole town apart. Even families." Sophie side-eyed her dad and then glared at Jeb. Great. Jeb was sending her on a roller coaster of emotions too, but hers were rolling between dislike and hate.

"What'll you have, kids?" Max slid a pen out from behind his ear and fished around in his apron pocket for a notepad.

Jeb cleared his throat, his face red. Sophie really knew how to make him uncomfortable. One step forward and two steps back. "A burger, medium-well, no onions, fries, and a double piece of blueberry pie."

"Ahh, my favorite. Helen Zauber dropped two off a few minutes ago. They're still warm. Emma?"

"Same, but a veggie burger and one piece of pie."

"Got it. Camilia?"

"Chicken tenders with barbeque sauce and a piece of pie to go."

"Sophie?"

"Veggie burger and sweet potatoes fries."

"Evelyn?"

"Same as Sophie."

"Great." He motioned behind the counter. "Grab some glasses, will you, Sophie? And clip this up for the guys in the back." He handed Sophie the ticket.

"I'll help you, Soph." Evelyn hopped up and followed her behind the counter.

No one called Sophie "Soph." And why was Evelyn eating the same thing as her? She wasn't a vegetarian. She usually got chicken tenders with barbeque like Cami. She was clearly trying to scoot into best-friend territory. It caused a weird feeling to slosh around my stomach.

Max leaned in closer to Jeb, his brown eyes serious. "Tell your dad there's going to be protesters at the zoning meeting."

Jeb nodded. "We know."

"Yeah. He's sitting with them," I said, crossing my arms. "The club and I are passing out flyers."

"Yeah," Cami said. "We've made signs."

Max's eyebrows shot up. "Oh. Thought maybe you'd come to your senses since you're spending so much time with Jeb."

"We're frenemies," Jeb laughed, clearing the tension. "She's trying to change my mind, and I'm trying to change hers."

Sophie and Evelyn came back to the table. Sophie handed me and Cami black cherry cream sodas and Jeb an empty cup. "I didn't know what you wanted," she said, her voice tight and edgy. She slid back into the booth, avoiding Jeb's eyes.

Max picked up Jeb's glass. "What'll you have, Jeb? I'll get it."

Suddenly, Paul's chair screeched against the floor. He jumped up from his table, almost knocking it over. The diner went still and quiet as everyone turned and stared. Paul glanced around and saw Jeb. The murderous look Paul gave Jeb made me shudder. He turned on his heel and stormed out of the diner.

"He still hates me," Max said. "Did you see that look he gave me?"

"Why does he hate you?" Sophie asked.

"Long story. Anyway, cream soda, Jeb? They make it locally at Black Mountain Soda Stream. It'd be great for the resort."

Jeb must have felt Paul's death glare too. He looked a little shook. "Um, sure."

"I've got vanilla, cane sugar, and black cherry at the fountain, but in bottles, I've got orange, blueberry, almond, butterscotch, maple cream, root beer, ginger, lime, jasmine, dandelion, white grape, apple—"

"Black cherry sounds great. Thanks," Jeb said.

Once Max left, I spoke up. "I think he was staring at you, Jeb. Not Max."

"Yep." Jeb's voice quivered. "If his eyes had been lasers, I'd be simmering on the ground right now."

Sophie nodded. "I know you guys think Mr. Zauber left those threats, but Paul's a more likely suspect."

"Soph's right," Evelyn said. "He's got a motive. Doesn't want to sell the land, and he obviously hates Jeb."

"But no one knows where Jeb is staying except us, my dad, and Mr. Zauber," I said.

Jeb started to say something but stopped when Max came to the table with his cream soda. "Your food will be out in a minute. Will you grab it when you see it in the window, Sophie?" Max pulled a straw out of his apron pocket and handed it to Jeb.

"Sure."

When Max left, Jeb leaned in and said quietly, "The notes were left inside the house. That's the creepiest part." He unwrapped the straw and stuck it in his soda.

"It is," Cami said. "How would Paul have gotten in?"

Sophie scowled at Jeb. "Do you really need a straw?"

Jeb rolled his eyes. "Are you even listening? You care more about the environment than my safety."

"Your dad got the threat, not you."

"Maybe, but I'm the one getting all the dirty looks. From Mr. Zauber, Paul, and you."

"What's that supposed to mean?" Evelyn asked. Her body got stiff, like she was ready for a fight.

Sophie looked ready to fight too. "Yeah. What are you getting at Jeb?"

"Nothing. Just facts. Stop looking at me like you wanna kill me."

I held up my hands like a traffic cop. "Guys, chill."

But Jeb was right. Sophie gave Jeb a lot of death glares. She wanted him gone. She knew where he stayed. She had a motive and means as much as anyone else.

"Your food's up, Sophie," Max said, as he passed by our table.

I'd known Sophie my whole life. There was no way she'd ever threaten anyone … but then again, I'd been wrong about a lot of things lately. My friendship with Sophie had been changing so gradually, I hadn't noticed how different it was until this week. Evelyn had been inching me out since she moved here. If I'd missed this, what else was I missing?

Chapter 12

Line: A mark made by a pointed object such as a brush, pen, or stick; a moving point

After lunch, we all split up. Jeb left with Tweedledum, Cami went to find Carlos and Alma, Evelyn went to the dance studio, and Sophie's dad made her stay and help in the restaurant. Sometimes, I helped too, but this afternoon, I had other plans. I wanted to find out more about Paul Cooper to cover all the angles in my investigation. I didn't know much about him. He'd moved away years ago, way before I was born. I sat on a bench in the town square and made a list of everything suspicious about him so I could connect the dots and see the big picture.

Number one: he had a good motive. He didn't want his land to be sold.

Number two: he had a temper. We saw how mad he'd gotten with Willa at the diner and the look he gave Jeb.

Number three: something wasn't right. Why would his dad leave everything to Willa? Where had he gone, and why was he back now after all these years?

I searched his name on my phone, but there were 478,000 results. It was a really common name. When I tried "Paul Cooper, Black Mountain, NC," the only thing that came up was an article about Paul's Peak on a hiker's blog. This was going to take old-school investigating. I was going to have to talk to people.

I decided to start with Erin, mostly because she was taking her lunch break in the square with Scout. She sat on the other side of the fountain, so I packed up my backpack and skated over to her. She smiled when she saw me, and Scout gave me a huge tail wag. I sat on my board next to Scout and scratched her ears. I made a little small talk with Erin, then I got right to it. "What do you know about Paul Cooper?"

Erin frowned. "Hmm ... it's been odd to see him after all this time. He came in the bookstore yesterday. I didn't recognize him at first."

"What did he want?"

"He asked about some books, but it seemed like he wanted to say hi and chat about what he'd been up to."

"What has he been up to?"

"Well, he travels a lot. He was married and lived in California, but now, he's divorced and lives in one of those conversion vans and travels all over the country. He says he's been doing it for years, way before it was cool."

"He doesn't have a job?"

"He has a blog with ads and a bunch of sponsors on social media. I've searched for him before, but I've never found him because he doesn't go by his name. It's a pseudonym, Joe Godspeed. He blogs about hiking, biking, traveling, and photography." She pulled out her phone and logged in to her Instagram. "Look how cool these are." She was right. He'd been everywhere. It looked like every national park from California to most recently the Great Smoky National Park, just past Asheville. His pictures were amazing. "He came back when he found out Willa was selling the land. He's really against it. His whole demeanor changed when he talked about it."

Now we were getting somewhere. "Like how?"

"His face got real red and ... well, I don't know. He always had a bad temper. It's why I broke up with him. Like the Incredible Hulk, you know? Sweet and nice one minute but ready to rip someone's head off the next. Figuratively, of course." She stared off for a second and then looked me in the eye. "Never date anyone with a temper."

"I won't."

"Good." Her face relaxed from dead serious to a silly grin. "By the way, I've seen you hanging out with that cutie-patootie Scott kid. What's that about?"

My face got hot. I leaned down and pet Scout so Erin wouldn't notice.

She must've, though, because she laughed. "Is he nice?"

I nodded. "Really nice." I scratched Scout under her chin, and she thumped her tail in appreciation. "He doesn't think Dad sent the death threat. He's helping me figure out who did."

"It definitely wasn't your dad," Erin said. "I can't believe anyone would even think that."

"Me too." I lowered my voice and glanced up at her. "Do you think Paul could've sent it?"

Erin looked thoughtful. "Honestly? I don't know. I mean, I can't imagine him actually hurting someone, but he was really mad—no, I don't think so. But we have police for that, Emma. You should let them handle it."

I nodded.

"Be careful." She zipped up her lunchbox and stood.

I gave Scout another hug and rolled myself out of their way. "Can I ask you one more thing?"

She gave me a sharp look but nodded.

"You said Paul was searching for books in your store. What was he looking for?"

"He wanted books about the Toggle Road Beast, which I thought was a strange coincidence since you asked me about that yesterday."

My heart stopped. Was Paul looking for me? He must've known I was on to him. "Did you tell him that?"

"I told him I had some but just sold them. Why?"

Relief flooded through me. I shrugged.

Erin looked like she could see right through me. "Like I said, be careful, Emma. The sheriff will figure everything out. You don't have to."

"I know."

She crossed back through the town square to her bookstore.

I let out a long breath and leaned back against the bottom of the bench. Why was Paul looking up the Toggle Road Beast? Maybe he'd been back on his property and heard it too.

I pulled out my tablet and typed in everything Erin had said. Paul was looking more and more like a possible suspect. I drew a line with my stylus from the numbers on my list to my notes. Erin had confirmed all my points. Things were definitely connecting. I saved the page and then opened a new one where I drew a huge question mark. I made a box for facts about Paul Cooper, a box for facts about Paul's Peak, and a box for the Death Threat.

Then, I opened up my Instagram app and clicked on Paul's travel page. His conversion van was awesome. It had wood paneling all over the inside, a little kitchen, a bed that could be changed into a seating area with a table, and even a little bathroom. Everything ran on solar power. He'd built the entire thing by hand. Impressive.

Before his van, he'd had a little camper, but he ditched it about six years ago. He had a bunch of ads for environmentally friendly stuff he used, like reusable water bottles with filters, blankets made with recycled plastic, biodegradable soap and toothpaste, sunglasses made of plant-based materials, tents, and a bunch of other gear made by companies that were certified animal-friendly and green. He didn't seem like a guy who would send death threats.

He'd traveled all over the West Coast, camping in the van and visiting national parks in California from Redwood to Yosemite, as well as Zion National Park and Bryce Canyon in Utah, Grand Canyon in Arizona, Yellowstone, a few more in Montana, Wyoming, and Colorado—

Wait. That sounded like … I pulled out the *Real Dog Men* book and flipped to the map.

Wowza. Wowza. Every place Paul had visited over the past ten years, there was a dog man sighting. Every. Place.

The book said one of the sightings was years ago in Asheville and, according to Erin, also near Paul's house around that same time. If he was three years older than Dad, he must've gone to college sometime after it'd been spotted. Now he was back … and so was the Toggle Road Beast.

Maybe *he* was the wolf, not Mr. Zauber. Maybe he was defending his family territory. His family had lived on that land for generations. Some of those headstones in the family cemetery were so old the names and dates were worn off. His ancestors could've been here even longer. Maybe twelve thousand years like Mrs. Bearpaw said. Maybe, like my green eyes, being able to change into a wolf was a recessive trait. Maybe it flowed through the generations, skipping a few but catching others. That painting in Mr. Zauber's barn could have been Paul's great-great-great grandfather or something.

It made more sense. My mind couldn't make the jump from Mr. Zauber, the corny old granddad, to Mr. Zauber, the vicious wolf, but Paul? That I could see. He'd practically snarled at his sister in the restaurant, and the death glare he gave Jeb had given me goosebumps. He seemed to really care about the environment. He could be trying to protect it by sending death threats and shifting into a vicious wolf. Maybe he was covering all the angles.

I copied a map onto a blank page on my tablet and dotted in the Dog Man sightings in red and Paul's travel post locations in black. I wrote the dates of sightings below the map and Paul's travel dates from his Instagram.

I texted Jeb. Hey, I found something!

Jeb: What?

Me: Paul Cooper has a travel Insta. Every place he's been over the past decade, there's been a Dog Man sighting documented in that book around the same time he's been there.

Jeb: What? You think Paul's the wolf?

I texted Jeb my map. Check this out.

Jeb: NO WAY!

Me: I know, right?

Across the street, Paul strolled along the sidewalk. He looked almost too casual, like he was trying to hide the fact he was a death-threat-sending-wolf-shifter. I texted Jeb, He just walked into our store. I'm going to follow him.

The sky was getting darker, like a storm was coming. Clouds rolled in across the tops of the mountains, closing in the town like a lid on a bowl. The warm breeze filled the square with the scent of the crepe myrtles blowing back and forth. Some of their flowers swirled to the ground. I skated through them and the little droplets from the fountain that splashed out in the wind.

The Walk light was on, so I kept going across the street, stopping in front of our hardware store. I kicked my board up to catch it like Jeb had, but it hit me in the shin and rolled away. I grabbed it off the sidewalk and went in.

The store was pretty empty, so it wouldn't be hard to find Paul. Dad was behind the counter. "Hey, kiddo! What's up?"

So, *so* much, but I didn't say that. "Not much. Sophie's helping Max, and I've been talking to Erin. I came in to see if I could get a cream soda."

"Sure. You know the drill." He pointed to the No Skateboards sign by the door.

I set my board behind the counter. Now it was time for part two of my investigation: surveillance. Paul was wearing a red baseball cap, gray T-shirt, and brown cargo shorts. He should be easy to spot.

I scanned the front of the store but didn't see him, so I started down the aisles. Our store was made up of three old shops. The first part had stuff for inside a person's home—everything from greeting cards to wind chimes to pots and pans to socks, soap, jelly, candy, and a ton of other random stuff. I went down each aisle. He wasn't there, so I crossed over to the middle hardware part. I didn't think he'd be in the toy section, so I skipped it. I cut through gardening supplies and went around the fishing equipment to the tools, and there he was, standing next to the knife case and looking at the axes that hung on the back wall.

I never understood why Dad sold so many axes. He'd tried to explain to me that each axe had a different purpose, but seriously, why did we need twenty rows of axes? There were a few really small ones with one stuck into a target to show how well you could throw it, other small ones you could hang on your belt, two-foot ones with blades covered in leather because they were so sharp, three-foot double-headed ones that looked like a weapon from a gladiator movie, and a bunch of sizes in between. It seemed like way too many, especially when people like Paul death-glaring-anger-issues-possible-death-threat-sending-might-be-the-Toggle-Road-Beast Cooper seemed to be very interested in the axes.

I stopped at the seed display near the axes and turned it slowly, pretending to look at the seeds, but really, I was studying him closely out of the corner of my eye. I could see him as a wolf. His beard was long and reddish-gray, and his hair poked out around his hat and down his neck. He turned and looked right at me. "Hey, I signed your petition." His voice was gruff and hoarse.

I thought I'd been incognito but evidently not. My heart beat so loud, I was sure he could hear it. I looked up from the seeds and tried to look surprised and confused.

"You're that kid from the ice cream place, right?" He pulled a two-foot axe down from the wall.

"Oh, right. Yeah. Thanks for doing that." I turned back to the seed display, pretending to be very interested in the orange milkweed.

"Didn't I see you at Max's with that Scott kid?" He checked out the sharpness of the axe blade by poking it with his finger.

"What?" Playing dumb was getting exhausting. I needed to move farther away to another aisle.

He nodded. "Yep, that was you. Why are you hanging out with him when you have a petition against his resort?"

Geez. Why was everybody so nosey? It was none of his business. I shrugged.

"Be careful who you hang out with." He shook the axe to test the grip—or was he threatening me? Fear fluttered through my chest. I wanted to scoot away, but my feet had suddenly turned to bricks. He sneered. "I mean, don't get too attached to that kid. He'll be leaving town soon."

Leave now or leave in a body bag later. I felt nauseous.

"You know, after the zoning meeting. When we win."

"I know what you mean."

"Hmm." He hung up the axe and picked up a smaller one. He faced the axe display and moved his arm forward in a throwing motion. "I'm thinking about opening a bar in that property next door to this store. One of those axe-throwing places. You seen those?"

"No."

"This one's perfect for throwing." He stared me in the eye. Beady amber eyes bugged out between his longish hair and scraggly beard. It didn't take much imagination to see him as the Toggle Road Beast.

The blood rushed loudly through my ears. My insides squeezed. I grabbed a packet of seeds, turned, and maneuvered quickly around the wheelbarrows through the fishing gear, past the paint, and through the key-making section. I stopped at the fridge full of Black Mountain Soda Stream Cream Sodas in the back of the store. I grabbed one and let out a little scream. Behind the soda was the missing doll from the dollhouse. She was wedged in the bin, staring with her creepy painted eyes. Geez. I took a couple of breaths to calm myself, then picked up the doll and headed to the register.

I'd never felt so relieved to see my dad. He was squatted down, reorganizing the pots and pans near the front of the store. He looked up when he heard me coming. "Are you okay?"

"This was in the back fridge," I said, handing him the doll. "It spooked me." I wanted to say, *Also, the Toggle Road Beast is checking out your axes,* but I kept that one to myself.

Dad laughed. "One of these days, I'm going to catch the kid who keeps doing this. It's a good prank."

"I know the kid who's doing it. She's dead."

Dad laughed again. "I love your imagination, honey," he said as he stood. "Are you planting tomatoes?"

"What?"

He pointed to the packet of seeds in my hand. I didn't realize I'd grabbed the tomato seeds.

"Oh. I grabbed the wrong thing. Can I leave them up here?" I motioned to the seed display I'd made in the front window last week.

"Sure."

"Okay. Great. And I took a ..." I looked down at the cream soda in my hand, "Cooper's Creek Cane Sugar. You want me to ring myself out?"

"Yeah, that'd be great."

"Good choice, kid. Cooper's Creek Cane Sugar is named after my family."

I jumped. Paul had walked up behind me. How did I not hear him? Maybe because wolf-shifters were stealthy.

"Are you ready, Paul? Emma can ring you out too."

Ugh. Seriously? I looked around the store. "Can't someone else? I gotta go."

Dad didn't even look up. "No, I asked you to do it. It will only take a second." He banged and knocked the cast iron skillets as he rehung him.

I walked over to the counter and went behind the register. Paul set down a little axe, the two-foot axe, some rope, a tarp, a big bag of beef jerky, and a Cooper's Creek Cane Sugar cream soda. I rang him up and put his stuff in a bag. As I handed it to him, I picked up my moonstone with my other hand and twisted so the light would reflect on him.

He stared, lizard-like, then blinked several times. "See you around, kid." He picked up his bags. "You might want to grab one of those umbrellas. Looks like a bad storm is coming," he said as he walked out of the store.

I let out my breath. What did he need all that stuff for? It didn't look good, and his reaction to the moonstone was weird. I rang up my cream soda, grabbed my board, and headed outside.

When I pulled out my phone, I had a couple of texts from Jeb. Be careful! And then: What happened? Everything okay?

I replied, He's sketchy for sure. I'm getting Sophie. Can you meet us at the fence between the Zaubers' and the Coopers'?

I was so preoccupied that I almost ran into Cami and Carlos as they walked by with Alma.

"Hey, qué pasa?" Carlos asked, smiling.

"Nada." I held out my soda to them. "Do you guys want this? I got the wrong flavor." I was never drinking Cooper's Creek Cane Sugar again.

"Sure, gracias!" Cami took it from me while Carlos flipped open his sketchbook.

"Check this out." He'd drawn the hardware store in graphite. The ghost of Eloise McCoy hovered by the door next to Arthur Fitzpatrick, the crooked-neck ghost who haunted the fountain.

"Creepy. What term is that?" I reached down and scratched Alma behind her ears. She put her head on my knees, which was her way of giving doggy hugs. She must have sensed how revved up I was.

"*Line*," Carlos said, "I thought it'd work because of all those horizontal and vertical lines on your store. What did you draw?"

I pulled out my tablet and clicked open the page with the lines connecting my points about Paul. It didn't count for my art journal project, but it definitely added up. "Tell your tío Sheriff Hernandez to investigate Paul Cooper. He's the one who sent the death threats, not my dad."

"¡Vaya! ¡Qué susto!" Cami said.

I nodded and put my hand on her arm. "I gotta talk to you. Can you come with me?"

"No, we're actually on our way to Tío Simon's house. I'll call you. Text me that chart. I'll show Tío Simon ASAP," Cami said.

I didn't mention my suspicion about the Toggle Road Beast since Carlos would've definitely thought I'd lost my mind. I said goodbye and crossed the street to the diner.

Max said Sophie was in the back, unpacking boxes of cups. I couldn't wait to tell her she'd been right about Paul. She loved being right. I weaved quickly around the tables, sped down the little hall past the kitchen, and burst through the storage room door. "You're never gonna believe what happened!" I yelled.

Sophie flinched and froze, holding a cup in midair. "Geez, you scared me!"

"Sorry, but I—"

"I thought you were mad at me."

I paused at the doorway. "What? Why?"

"For giving Jeb death glares."

Oh. I'd been so caught up in investigating Paul, I completely forgot about the whole exchange at lunch. "No, I'm not mad. I've been following Paul. I think you're right. I think it was him, not Mr. Zauber."

"I was actually trying to be nice to Jeb at the garden," she said as she took more cups out of the box, "but he's impossible."

"I know." I walked over and grabbed a package of cups and placed them on the shelf next to Sophie's. We used to see who could stack them the highest, until my stack crashed all over the storage room, and Max lectured us for being irresponsible. Now we stack them carefully, about twenty cups high.

Sophie set the cups on the shelf a little harder than necessary. "Ever since Jeb came, all you want to do is hang out with him."

"That's not true." Well … maybe it was a little true, but I wasn't going to admit it. "Besides, *you* just want to hang out with Evelyn."

"That's not fair! You could hang out with us too, but you're too busy hanging out with Jeb. You don't even answer my texts."

"Yes, I do."

"I texted you the other night to see if you wanted to sleep over, but you ignored me. Cami answered. She couldn't. Evelyn said yes."

"You did?"

I pulled out my phone and scrolled through my messages. Yep, she'd texted me right before I went out with Jeb that first night when we got ice cream by the fountain. Maybe she had a point. This whole time, I thought she was ditching me, but I was the one who'd accidentally ghosted her. That was why she'd been so mad.

"I'm sorry. I totally missed your text. I guess I've been distracted. I'm really worried about my dad and a little freaked out that there's a possible murderer loose in town." I placed the last cup from my package on the stack and faced her. "We've got to prove Dad didn't send that threat. That's what I've been working on all afternoon. I need your help. You're my best friend, Sophie. You'll always be my best friend, no matter what."

"Promise?"

"Yes."

She smiled, and her shoulders relaxed. "You'll always be my best friend too. No matter what."

While we unloaded the rest of the box, I told her all about Paul—without all the Toggle Road Beast details, of course. We decided to start our search on the Coopers' property to see if Paul was camping there and to search for the wolf. Sophie still thought it was to show the EPA, but I still needed to clear Dad. Whoever was the Toggle Road Beast—Paul or Mr. Zauber—we'd catch them, and they'd admit who they were and what they'd done. It was the only way to clear Dad.

※ ※ ※

When we walked out of the diner, the clouds above town were completely black. It started sprinkling before we reached the trail. We skated faster. The cool rain hitting my face felt good, but then, thunder shook the ground, the sky opened up, and it poured. As lightning flashed, we picked up our boards and ran the rest of the way to my house.

It didn't let up, so Sophie's brother, Zac, met us in my driveway and picked her up. I hurried inside and up to my room, where I changed out of my soggy clothes and put my wet hair up in a high bun. Then, I video-chatted Jeb and Cami. I told them every detail about my run-in with Paul. Jeb agreed to meet up at the Coopers' tomorrow. But tomorrow was the zoning meeting. I was running out of time.

Chapter 13

Contrast: the difference between elements like value, color, shape, or line

It was still storming in the morning. I paced back and forth across my bedroom floor, my mind whirling with visions of my run-in with Paul, the wolf tracks, and flowers being ripped out of the ground by bulldozers.

To calm myself, I worked on the design for Jeb's skateboard. I wanted something different from his Jesse Marxx, something better. I drew four triangular mountain peaks in thick black lines with clouds behind them. Not fluffy ones. I drew them with sharp lines and angles. Then, I drew a huge oval for the sun. I filled in the sky with yellow, the clouds orange, and the sun and ground red-orange.

I took a picture with my tablet to send to Jeb. Then, I added the drawing to my art terms journal for the word *contrast*. That was the word of the day. It seemed like everyone in town had contrasting ideas about what was best for the town. I couldn't believe we had to fight so hard to keep the ski resort away. I'd really thought we'd all be on the same side. I'd never been so wrong in my life.

Right when I finished, Sophie video-chatted me. Her face was bright and excited. "We got permission from the commissioner for us to speak at the zoning meeting!"

A wave of nausea hit me.

"This is our chance! They'll listen to us, Emma."

I wasn't so sure.

She discussed talking points, but I wasn't paying attention. I couldn't do it, especially not with Jeb sitting in front of me.

"Hello? Hello? Earth to Emma?"

"Yeah ... I-I'm listening."

"No, you're not," Sophie said with a sigh. "I know you're nervous, but channel your inner Greta. Remember her 'How Dare You!' speech. It was phenomenal!" She cleared her throat. "You have stolen my dreams and my childhood with your empty words," she recited in her best Greta Thunberg impersonation. "And yet I'm one of the lucky ones. People are suffering. People are dying. Entire ecosystems are collapsing." Her voice got louder. "We are in the beginning of mass extinction, and all you can talk about is money and fairy tales of eternal economic growth." She raised her fist and yelled, "How dare you!"

"The eyes of all future generations are upon you," I recited. "And if you choose to fail us, I say: We will never forgive you! We will not let you get away with this. Right here, right now is where we draw the line." My Greta impersonation was not as good as Sophie's, but I gave it my all.

Sophie cheered. "It gives me goosebumps every time I hear it."

I smiled, feeling slightly better. "Me too."

"We can do this, Emma. We have to. Now's our chance to change everyone's mind—Jeb's, the commissioner's ... my dad's." Her face fell. "I still can't believe my dad's such a sellout. He really thinks I'll cave when he makes more money at the diner."

"It's not his fault. Greta's right. It's not only your dad. People believe what they want to believe. They only see what they want to see." I wanted to add, *Like you not believing the wolf we saw wasn't a normal wolf.* Instead, I continued, "Greta was talking to the United Nations Climate Action Summit. People that were supposed to be on our side, but they weren't, really. You can't blame your dad for being any different. And we can't blame Jeb either. Nobody's listening."

Sophie nodded. "You're right. We have to show them. Like you tried to do yesterday with Jeb. Show them why it's important not just to us but to them too. I'm coming over."

Zac dropped her off a few minutes later. She stood on my porch, a monarch perched upside down on her finger. It must have just hatched because its wings were crumpled and still. "It's time for show-and-tell," Sophie said, smiling as she held up the bag in her other hand.

We went up to my bedroom and put together our plan for the zoning meeting. I agreed to speak but only if I could go second, so I could stop if I needed to. My main job would be to hold up our visuals. I'd be mostly "show," and Sophie would be all "tell." Kind of like our personalities.

It poured all afternoon, right up until the time Miss Bettie came over to watch Addie. We'd have to go to the Coopers' after the meeting to find the Toggle Road Beast, win or lose.

When we got to the courthouse, Cami, Carlos, and Evelyn were already there. They'd passed out our protest signs to a few kids and adults. "Hey, hey, ho, ho! Chester Scott has got to go!" they all chanted.

I set our show-and-tell box down on the sidewalk next to them. It was still closed for the dramatic reveal. Sophie and I passed out flyers, but Mom and Dad went inside since Dad was trying to keep a low profile. I didn't see how anyone could think he'd threatened Chester Scott, but I couldn't be sure about anyone in our town anymore.

Most of the people going into the courthouse took a flyer. Some threw them away in the garbage as they walked in. Others smiled and stuffed them in their pockets or purses without reading them. A few stopped to chat briefly and thank us for our hard work. Some shook their heads or avoided eye contact completely.

Jeb arrived five minutes before the meeting was supposed to start. The black SUV pulled up to the curb, and Tweedledum hopped out, followed by Chester and Jeb. He smiled when he saw me. He wore khakis and a forest-green dress shirt with the sleeves partially rolled up. His hair was perfectly in place. Ugh. I took a few deep breaths and blew them out to calm myself. I could do this. I'd just needed to keep my eyes focused on the back of the room and not look at Jeb. Sophie tried to get around Tweedledum and hand Chester a flyer, but she was quickly cut off.

The turnout was huge. There were so many people, Sophie and I had to squeeze through the crowd to the back entrance. Mom and Dad sat at a table near the front with Cami's dad and some others from the Monarch Project. Jeb and his dad sat at a table across from them on the other side of the aisle. Erin let us squish in next to her on the bench near the back of the courthouse. I set the box down gently under my feet.

The zoning board members sat in front of the courtroom on an elevated stage behind a long, semicircular table. Behind them hung the town seal. I'd seen it before but never that big. It was about four feet in diameter with dark-blue mountains in the background and one tree in the forefront behind the lake. The words *Town of Black Mountain* circled the outside. The date 1893 was at the bottom. With a seal like that, the zoning board would never let someone come in and tear up a mountain. We were Black *Mountain*, after all.

The chair, Rush Lightfoot, sat in the middle. He was Stella Bearpaw's cousin and Cherokee too, so I knew he was 110 percent against the ski resort. But he'd have to be professional and not show which side he was on. "Ladies and gentlemen," he said, "we're going to begin the meeting of the Black Mountain Zoning and Planning Commission, and I would like to open the agenda with having the roll call taken."

The five commissioners, sitting around the table, said, "Here," after he called out each of their names. Sophie's dad was one of them. She tensed up next to me when Commissioner Lightfoot called his name. Mr. Zauber was a commissioner too. He still had the bandage on his head. The other three were Mr. Corrado, Mrs. Rockwell, and Mrs. Washington. I didn't know them very well, so I couldn't predict how they'd vote, but Mrs. Washington was Mrs. Hartford's sister-in-law. Surely, she'd be on our side.

"We have a quorum," Commissioner Lightfoot said. "That quorum will allow us to continue with the agenda that we have before us tonight. And I perceive some of you sitting before me in the courtroom are here for the voting part of the process, and you may want to speak." He cleared his throat and looked around the room at everyone. "You'll see on the agenda that members of the public will be allowed testimony for five minutes. You will be timed. If there are no questions, let's get to it, Commissioner Jones."

I tingled all over. I really, *really* didn't want to speak.

Max leaned toward the microphone. "This is case no. 18 P-04, a request for a rezoning of ninety acres of land at 1222 Black Mountain Road. The applicant is Chester Scott. He proposes to build a yet unnamed ski resort, including five ski runs, a chairlift, a fifteen-story hotel, gift shop, ski lodge with a restaurant, and ten ski chalets. The land is currently zoned for a single dwelling property. Mr. Scott, you may have the floor."

"Thank you, Commissioner Jones." Chester dramatically pulled off the sheets of fabric covering drawings of the resort. It looked fancy, like something you'd see in Switzerland. A few people in the crowd gasped. Chester smiled, and in his best narrator voice—the one he'd used in all those coffee commercials—described the resort and all the benefits it would bring Black Mountain. It was basically the same spiel Jeb had given me and Sophie when we first met him but with a little bit more flash. The people sitting in the courthouse followed his every move like they were watching the most interesting play they'd ever seen. When he was finished, they clapped.

"Thank you, Mr. Scott," Commissioner Lightfoot said. "Now we'll hear from Dr. Murry and Dr. Suárez, the representatives from the Monarch Larva Butterfly Project."

I leaned forward on the bench. Mom was a natural. She was so good at public speaking. I crossed my fingers and made a little wish that it would rub off on me. She was wearing her best professor outfit with the monarch butterfly brooch on her lapel. "Thank you, Chairman Lightfoot and members of the commission. As you know, I'm the liaison between the National Monarch Larva Project based out of the University of Wisconsin, and Dr. Suárez is the liaison with Mexico's Commission for Natural Protected Areas. We, along with our students, have partnered with the community of Black Mountain to create a butterfly utopia on our greenway. I'm appreciative of the enthusiasm members of the town have brought to our project. These include the Black Mountain Middle School Environmental Club at Black Mountain Middle School under the leadership of their principal Dr. McGuire; the Black Mountain Kiwanis, of which several of our commissioners are members; the Parks and Recreation, who help sponsor our festival every year; the Black Mountain Garden Club; and many, many members of our community. We have all worked together to create a state-of-the-art garden that has had a marked impact on butterfly migration."

"As you can see," Cami's dad said as he placed a graph on the easel, "we've tracked thousands of Black Mountain monarchs all the way to Mexico." He pointed to the graph. "This is twenty-five percent more than the other stations across the county. The support here in Black Mountain is very important to the success of the whole butterfly project."

"That's right," Mom said. "As pollinators, monarchs are essential for ecosystems to thrive. Our meadow provides a safe area for them to lay their eggs on milkweed—which, as you know, is the only place they will lay eggs. All of the support of this community has had a direct impact on the fate of monarchs in the world. That should make each and every one of us proud. The destruction of the garden and part of the meadow would be devastating to our cause. In addition, the butterflies roost in the trees on Paul's Peak as part of their migration path. Destroying the mountain would change their migration patterns, and many of them will die."

Dr. Suárez switched to a different graph. This one was titled *Presence of monarch butterflies in Mexican hibernation forests deceased by 26% last December.* "We are in an unprecedented time of climate change," he said. "It's had a considerable impact on the monarchs' migration process. Last spring and summer, the climate changes in the South caused less milkweed to grow in many areas. This led to fewer eggs being laid and hatched, causing a smaller population hibernating in the Mexican forests." He gestured toward the graph. It showed how butterfly colonies were way smaller this year than last year.

He moved that graph and put another poster up. "Mexico, Canada, and the US are aware of the major challenges we face. They are"—he cleared his throat—"number one: the reduction of breeding sites because of a decrease in milkweed in the US. Number two: forest degradation in hibernation sites in Mexico and land use in the United States. And number three: extreme weather. We all must double down on our efforts to work together to confront these situations that threaten these beautiful butterflies' journey and reproduction. That starts right here in Black Mountain by preserving our garden and Paul's Peak."

"Exactly," Mom said. "While we support economic development, we and many members of our community do not support development at the cost of the monarchs, something our area is known for. The garden and the festival already bring in up to thirty thousand people and have a positive impact on the town economy. We're presenting a petition to you, signed by members of the community, asking for your recommendation to maintain the current zoning at 1222 Black Mountain Road as a single dwelling home."

Hooray, Mom! She was amazing.

"Thank you," Commissioner Lightfoot said. "Are there any questions from the commission?"

The only commissioner who looked at Mom and Cami's dad was Mr. Zauber. The others avoided eye contact, but he leaned forward. "Dr. Murry and Dr. Suárez, I would like to thank you for your commitment to our community and the environment. My question is: How many signatures do you have on your petition?"

Mom smiled. "One thousand five hundred and fifty signatures."

"Okay, thank you very much," Commissioner Lightfoot said. "This will be Interested Party Exhibit no. 1." He cleared his throat and looked out at the crowd. "How many people out there, by a raising of hands, are wanting to speak?"

Sophie and several people raised their hands. She elbowed me. I swallowed, trying to get the rock-sized lump out of my throat, and raised my hand too.

"Okay. We'll start left to right. Remember, I said earlier that when you're called upon, you will be given five minutes."

Sophie and I had practiced. I only had to talk two minutes, but that was going to feel like an eternity.

Max came down and stood next to the podium on the side of the room. It was angled so the person speaking could face the commissioners and the people sitting in the audience. "Okay.

We'll take the first person. Speak to the commission and give us your input."

Dr. McGuire, the principal at my school, spoke first. She asked that the board vote yes because the increase in property tax would help fund the school system. She explained how the overcrowded middle school currently had the entire eighth grade outside in trailers, and so they needed to build a new wing. They also needed to update the computer system.

Whoa. That was unexpected. Dr. McGuire loved the butterfly garden. She was part of the project, and she'd helped the Environmental Club plant milkweed around the school. Sophie and I were pumped to be in a trailer next year. We didn't want to be stuck inside the school. We'd have our own hangout area in the trailer courtyard with benches and a couple of tree swings. Why would Dr. McGuire destroy everything so we could be in that crappy old building?

Next, our neighbor, Mrs. Adair, spoke about the impact all the traffic would have on Black Mountain Road and the roads around it. She described how it would be unsafe for neighborhood kids to play outside on the street and talked about how the greenway provided a safe way for kids to get into town. It was nice to know someone was thinking about us.

Mr. Cho, the chair of the Black Mountain Tourism Development Authority Board, spoke next. He presented a study about how good the butterfly garden and festival were for the town's economy. I was sure he'd had good points, but my nerves started getting to me, and I tuned him out. Jeb wasn't listening either. He was scrolling through his phone.

More people from town popped up and spoke one by one. Every time it got closer to my turn, the rock in my throat got bigger and bigger, and I couldn't focus on what they were saying. I forced my body to stay in my seat, but I really wanted to run out the door.

Then, Commissioner Lightfoot called on me and Sophie. The rock in my throat twisted and turned. I felt sick.

I picked up the box, and Sophie grabbed her backpack. The people on our row stood and moved out of the way into the aisle so Sophie and I could get by. They smiled reassuringly at us. Sophie looked smug and confident like the *Mona Lisa*. I probably looked like *The Scream* by Edvard Munch.

Max had us sign in at the podium. He wouldn't look us in the eye. I set the box down as Sophie moved the mic down to our level. It let off a little squeak, and I jumped. My heart was beating so loud, it was the only thing I could hear. Sophie elbowed and smiled at me. This was my cue to remove our surprise from the box: the glass butterfly terrarium. It had orange butterfly weed, some white milkweed, and the three caterpillars and two butterflies we'd found that afternoon.

Just about everybody smiled at us. Mom's smile was the biggest. She gave me a reassuring nod, sending her ultraviolet comforting mom rays over me. She was right. I knew almost everyone in the crowd. I could do this.

Sophie pulled a container out of her backpack. "Do you love Mrs. Zauber's blueberry pie?" she asked, looking at Jeb and popping the lid of the container.

She handed it to me, and I took it to him. He laughed as he took it. His hand brushed my thumb, sending little jolts of electricity up my arm. I pictured him snowboarding on the treeless mountain to keep my focus.

"Or maybe the Black Cherry cream soda from Black Mountain Soda Stream?" Sophie asked, handing me a cardboard carton with six bottles. I passed one out to each member of the zoning board.

"Or maybe my dad's barbeque?" She took a container of mini sandwiches out of the cooler. I passed them out to the board too and then handed the container to Blair. She took one and passed the container down the row. *Everyone* smiled at us now.

Sophie smiled back at them. "I see that you do! As you enjoy these delicious treats, be sure to thank a pollinator. Without pollinators, none of these would be possible. In fact, without pollinators, the human race and all of earth's terrestrial ecosystems wouldn't survive. The garden, meadow, and mountain are home to several pollinators—bees, butterflies, birds, and beetles. Most crops rely on insects and birds to move pollen grains between plants so they can have seeds and fruit. One out of every three bites of food you eat everyday are there because of pollinators."

"Alcohol too," I said. My voice sounded scratchy, so I cleared my throat and forced a smile. "Like the wine from Antonia's and the margaritas from Taco Heaven. We couldn't bring those. You'll have to get them for yourselves." I tried to sound peppy and happy.

Everyone chuckled, making me relax a little more. Jeb looked up from his pie and winked at me. I ignored my kickflipping stomach and focused on Sophie.

"Like Emma's mom said—" Sophie let out a nervous giggle, "I mean, like Dr. Murry said, our meadow's most celebrated resident pollinator is the monarch. They pollinate flowers that can only be reached by their long proboscis—or nose. Since they migrate, they pollinate a wider geographic range compared to bees. Their extinction would impact many different wild plants. That's one reason our town has embraced this beautiful insect."

"That's not the only reason." My voice came out way too high. I took a deep breath and looked at Dad. He smiled, sending me his teal waves of confidence. "We've also embraced the monarch, the garden, and the meadow because of their beauty." Good, my voice sounded more normal now. "You're all very smart." I forced my eyes from Dad and scanned the crowd. They all stared at me kindly and intently. "You understand the environmental impact of losing the garden and the meadow, but I don't think you've thought enough about the beauty that will be lost."

I picked up the terrarium and moved out from behind the podium. "Biological treasures are as valuable as great works of art. For centuries, people have worked hard to preserve and protect art. People value and appreciate Monets, van Goghs, da Vincis, and so many others. But here in our town, we have our own great work of art. A living, breathing, beautiful garden and meadow inhabited by one of the most beautiful butterflies on earth. You can't put a price on beauty. Monarchs are going extinct. You know this. It is our job as humans to protect them."

I walked down the aisle, keeping my eyes on the terrarium, but I could see the heads in the crowd move and follow me as I walked. "My family has lived in Black Mountain for generations. One day, I hope I can walk on the greenway with my granddaughter. I'll point out the butterfly weed, the milkweed, the purple coneflower, Shasta daisies, hydrangeas, and all the other flowers and bushes. Butterflies will flit around us." I moved back up the aisle and stopped in front of Jeb and Chester. "We'll stop and watch the incredible transformation of caterpillar to chrysalis. Then, I'll tell her about a time some famous guys came to our town and tried to destroy everything that was beautiful." I looked Jeb dead in the eye. He froze with his forkful of pie dangling in front of his open mouth. I turned to the commissioners. "I hope I can tell her you chose to save it."

Most of the commissioners stared at me blankly except for Mr. Zauber. He was beaming. He stood and clapped. Mr. Lightfoot caught my eye and winked. Cami, Carlos, and Evelyn stood and whooped. Mom and Dad stood too, looking very proud. So did Cami's dad, Mrs. Bearpaw, Erin, and Mrs. Hartford, who also gave a little cheer. A lot people stood and clapped but not everyone. I didn't look at Jeb as Sophie and I went back to the bench.

Hot tears burned my eyes. I wasn't sure if it was from sadness, happiness, or relief to be done speaking. My emotions were swirling around like a tornado. I knew I loved the garden, meadow, and mountain, but right then, I knew I loved them more than *anything*. I couldn't like Jeb if he didn't care about what I loved the most. Erin gave Sophie and me a hug before we sat down. I leaned into her and hugged her back.

"You were phenomenal," Sophie whispered in my ear. "Just like Greta." It was the highest compliment she could've given. My whole body soared with relief and happiness, like I'd climbed to the highest peak and flew off like an eagle.

"You were amazing too," I whispered back as I put my arm around her and squeezed.

Blair was called on next. I scooted forward on the bench, sure that after hearing our testimony, she would change her mind. She made her way to the podium, cleared her throat, and read from a note card. "Thank you for giving us this opportunity to present our comments and concerns. I know that some members of the community, who I hold dear to my heart, are opposed to the rezoning of the Cooper property, but—"

"That's my property, and I'm not selling!" Paul Cooper stomped into the courthouse from the side door, slamming it behind him. Every head snapped in his direction.

"It's not your property!" Willa jumped up, and everyone looked at her. "I'm the controlling member of the LLC. It's mine! You *know* that, Paul."

"Please!" Commissioner Lightfoot said, standing. "Ms. Geller-Reynolds has the floor."

Paul went on like he hadn't been interrupted. "You know Pop didn't want this! He wanted to preserve the beauty of the mountain so other kids could have what we had, Willa."

"Paul!" Mr. Lightfoot was yelling now. "If you don't sit down and wait your turn, you'll have to leave!"

Paul moved forward to the front of the room. "That's my peak where this resort is going. It's named after *me*!" His face was red and contorted. I held my breath, waiting for the buttons to pop off his shirt as his furry wolf body spilled out.

"It's mine, Paul!" Willa yelled back.

Heads in the courtroom snapped back and forth like they were watching a tennis match. I kept my eyes on Paul.

"Paul! Willa! Ms. Geller-Reynolds has the floor. Sit down!" Commissioner Lightfoot yelled. His face was tomato-red.

Sheriff Hernandez moved from the corner. Paul quickly sat in Blair's spot on the bench next to Matt, who frowned like he'd eaten a sour blueberry, sighed loudly, and scooted away. Paul was breathing hard. His back moved up and down quickly. He leaned forward and put his hands on his forehead and his elbows on his knees.

"I'm sorry for the interruption, Ms. Geller-Reynolds." Commissioner Lightfoot sighed as he sat back down. "You may continue."

Blair rocked from foot to foot, looking at Paul like she wanted to push him off the bench. She sighed. "Okay. Where was I? Oh, yes. I, along with several other business owners in our community, believe the resort will boost our town economy during the slow months of the winter ..."

I was too distracted by Paul to listen to Blair. I was sure that Paul would turn into the wolf any minute. His breathing was fast and his shoulders were tense, but whatever relaxation technique he used must've really worked because he didn't turn into a wolf.

Blair continued to babble on and on. I silently wished Paul would turn into the wolf and shut her up, but then I felt bad. I loved Blair; she was great. So why was she being such a traitor?

"... for choosing our town to build his fabulous resort." Blair beamed at Chester as she clapped.

"Thank you, Ms. Geller-Reynolds. How many signatures are on your petition?"

"Three thousand five hundred and sixty-eight."

I almost fell off the bench. Sophie went limp. Who were they? Could Erin have been one? I turned toward her. She squeezed my hand. "I'm on your side, remember?" she whispered as if she'd read my mind.

"Thank you," said Commissioner Lightfoot. "This will be Interested Party Exhibit no. 2. At this time, we'll close the public hearing, and the commissioners will vote. We'll return after a brief intermission and inform the public of our decision." Commissioner

Lightfoot stood and went out through the door behind the table. The other commissioners followed.

Blair walked back to her spot on the bench, and Paul hopped up so she could sit down. He went and leaned against the wall by the door, his face still red.

Mom and Dad turned and looked through the crowd. I gave them a little wave. They both smiled, and Dad gave me a thumbs-up. I was hopeful we'd get the votes we needed. Max would vote for the rezoning, but even though Blair had more signatures, more people from our side spoke. So many people were against the ski resort, I didn't see how the commissioners could vote any other way. Chairman Lightfoot was on our side and so was Mr. Zauber. They'd both lived in Black Mountain a long time, and a lot of people respected them. They'd convince whoever was on the fence. They had to.

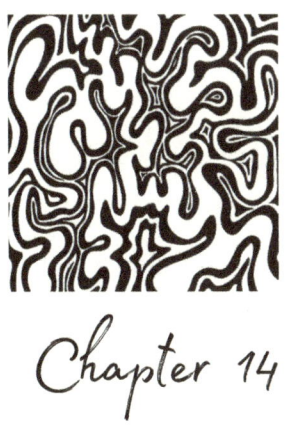

Chapter 14

Movement: used to create the look and feeling of action in the artwork

It only took fifteen minutes. The commissioners came out of the back room and took their seats. They kept their heads down. No one seemed to want to make eye contact with the crowd.

"Mr. Jones, please read the board's decision," Commissioner Lightfoot said.

Max stood. "The board has reviewed case no. 18 P-04, a request for a rezoning of ninety acres of land at 1222 Black Mountain Road. After careful consideration of all the evidence presented today, the board has voted four to two in favor of the rezoning."

The courtroom erupted. There were a few gasps and cries of "no." Some people cheered. Paul stormed out.

I felt dizzy. Little brown squiggles spun in front of me around the courtroom. It was like my mixing tray had flipped over, and everyone's color swirled together with Jeb's ugly gray. Mr. Zauber's sunshine yellow, Sophie's crimson, Dad's ocean teal, Blair's sugary white, Matt's blueberry, Erin's shimmery forest green, Mrs. Hartford's purple, all spinning in an ugly murky poop-colored brown. Mom's ultraviolet could not protect me anymore. I sat, stunned.

Sophie jumped up and ran down the aisle toward the door. Erin looped her arm around me and squeezed. "I … I gotta find Sophie," I said, sliding out from under her arm and picking up the box. I worked my way through the crowd to the hallway. I felt like I was walking down a long dark tunnel full of strangers.

By the time I reached the sidewalk, Sophie was gone. I stood mixed in the sea of people spilling out of the courthouse. I felt like a fish out of water. Most were talking excitedly, smiling and laughing. The crowd parted when Chester and Jeb came out. Some even clapped as they went by. Jeb looked around and caught my eye, giving me a thumbs-up. My hair tie dangled from his wrist. A sharp pain exploded in my stomach, like he'd punched me. I quickly turned away and maneuvered my way out of the crowd. My phone buzzed in my pocket.

It was Jeb.

This whole time, I'd thought I could change his mind, and he'd believed I'd change mine. He thought once the ski resort was open, I'd be okay with it. But I never would. I loved the mountain, garden, and meadow. I loved the sweet smells, the bright colors, and the butterflies that flitted around. But this was bigger than me and what I loved. Forest animals, monarchs, and other insects would have no place to go. A stupid ski resort wasn't worth it. Jeb wasn't worth it.

Sophie had been right all along. My googly eyes had not focused on what was important. I'd been so distracted by a cute guy with a cool skateboard, I believed I could change his mind. I actually thought he liked me. How dumb. He only cared about himself.

I didn't read his message. I slid my thumb across my screen, deleting it and every text he'd ever sent. Then, I put my phone on silent and blocked his number.

Cami, Evelyn, and Carlos came up to me. They still held our signs. "We're not giving up yet, right?" Cami said. "We're going to protest. Every day until they're so sick of us they leave."

"Definitely." Evelyn shook a poster high in the air. "We can be like Greta. We'll come every day and won't let them forget."

Mom spotted us and walked over. She gave me a huge hug. "I'm so sorry it didn't go our way."

My tears welled, making everything blurry. "How could they vote for the resort? After everything we told them and showed them? How could they not care?"

"I know this has been very hard for you," Mom said. She pointed to the box with the terrarium. "It's got me thinking. Growing up is a lot like the stages of the monarch butterfly."

"What?" Mom needed to get out of the lab more. She wasn't making sense.

She smiled a tired smile. "I'm not crazy. Hear me out." She put her arm around my shoulders and steered me toward the parking lot. "When you're a little kid, like Addie, your whole world is centered around your family. You don't venture too far away from them, not only in your location, but also mentally—as in your thoughts and ideas. You're in your own little world like the caterpillar who only lives and eats on milkweed. Then, as you get older and become a teenager—"

"All you want to do is wrap yourself up in a hoodie and hide under your covers like a pupa," I said as we stopped at our car.

Mom laughed lightly and gave my shoulders a little squeeze. "Well, sort of. Everything starts to change. All the physical stuff, of course, which is more obvious and everyone talks about, but there's a whole lot more that happens." She paused as she opened the door.

I crossed my arms across my chest. Surely, she wasn't going to jump into a puberty discussion now.

Mom slid into the driver's seat, and I slid in the seat behind her. "You venture out into the world more," she continued, "you develop your own ideas, and you meet new people who influence everything. All of your old experiences stay with you, but you also form into a new version of yourself, an older, wiser version where you realize the world is not as simple as you thought it was. All of these ideas and experiences can make you feel like you're turning into mush. It might even be painful."

She turned around and faced me. "Right now, you're stuck, like the butterfly that emerges with crumpled and wet wings and has to dry off and straighten out. You're realizing that people are complicated, and the world doesn't always make sense. But eventually, your wings will dry, and you'll fly off as the most beautiful butterfly," Mom said as she buckled her seatbelt. "You were terrific today. You're an intelligent and passionate young lady—a world-changer, and I can't wait to see what you do next."

"Thanks, Mom." I didn't feel terrific. I felt like the whole world was crashing down on top of me. My body ached with anger and sadness. I felt more like I was in the pupa stage, turning into mush. If this was what it meant to grow up, I'd rather be a kid.

Sophie opened the door and collapsed into the seat next to me. Her eyes were watery and bloodshot, and her face was pale and splotchy. "I can't believe our whole town sucks so bad."

"I know."

"We have to get a picture of that wolf," she whispered. "It's our only hope. It could change everything."

I nodded.

Dad finally showed up right before the rain started. "You guys were awesome," he said, turning to face me and Sophie. "I'm very proud of both of you."

Mom drove off through the mostly empty parking lot. Our ride back home was quiet except for the squeak of the windshield wipers going back and forth. Mom didn't drop Sophie off at her dad's house, and no one reminded her. I doubted Sophie wanted to go back to his house yet. Or ever, really.

As we pulled into our driveway and hopped out of our car, a police car pulled in behind us. Sheriff Hernandez got out and flashed his badge. "I'm really sorry about this, Jimmy."

"Sorry about what?"

"You're under arrest."

"What? Why?"

"For terroristic threatening." Sheriff Hernandez looked at Mom. "Andrea, call your lawyer and meet us at the station." He took a little handkerchief out of his pocked and dabbed the rain on his face. "I'm sorry, but Jimmy, I also have to ask you if you know where Jeb Scott is."

"Simon," Dad's voice cracked, "you've known me for years. You know I'd never—"

"What do you mean? Where's Jeb?" I asked, heart racing. "Is he missing?"

"He told his dad he'd be right back but never showed up, and he's not answering his phone. It's been almost an hour. His family is very worried."

"We just left the courthouse. Everyone did," Mom said. "You can't possibly think Jimmy had anything to do with—"

"Were you with him the whole time?"

"No, but Simon, you know as well as I—"

"It doesn't matter what I think. I have to do my job. I don't wanna cuff you, Jimmy. Not in front of the kids. So get in the back, okay?"

Dad's green eyes were huge and round, and his face was pale. He tried to look brave as he hugged Mom and then ducked into the back of the sheriff's car, but I could tell he was really worried.

Mom gave the Sheriff a sharp glare. "Really, Simon? Jeb's only been gone an hour. He's probably skating somewhere on the greenway."

"Jimmy's a suspect for terroristic threating. That's all, but if something happens to that kid ... well, just call your lawyer. Now."

"You can't have any evidence. He didn't do it!" Mom yelled. I'd never seen her that angry.

Sheriff Hernandez opened the door to his car. "I'm sorry. I really am," he said, sliding into his seat. He slammed the door shut and backed out of the driveway.

Mom jumped back in our car. "Tell Bettie what's going on. I'll be back as soon as I can." Sophie and I moved out of her way as she threw the car into reverse and sped off down the road.

"I didn't think things could get any worse," Sophie said.

"We're gonna go to the Coopers'," I said, running up to the house. "I'm getting Dad's camera and a picture of the wolf. We're gonna end this thing right now!"

Sophie followed behind me, carrying the box with the butterfly terrarium. I threw open the front door and ran upstairs, skipping every other step. I raced into Mom and Dad's room and grabbed the camera from the top shelf of their closet. It would work better than my phone when it got dark. I could up the exposure and catch the Toggle Road Beast, even if it ran. Then, I ran into my room and grabbed one of the squirt guns with the wolfsbane water and stuck it in my back pocket. I reached up and felt my neck for the moonstone necklace. I still had it on. Good.

Sophie stayed downstairs and explained what was going on to Miss Bettie, who didn't seem to be comprehending. "What? The sheriff? You mean Simon? Did what now?" she asked.

I ran into the kitchen. "They arrested Dad. Mom went with him."

Bettie fell onto the stool at the counter. "Oh, Lord … you gonna tell Addie, or should I?"

"Can you? Sophie and I are going out. You can stay late, right? I might spend the night with Sophie."

"Going out where? Why do you have the camera?"

"We're taking pictures of nature. I'm still trying to convince Jeb to give up on the ski resort idea." My heart was pounding, and I could hardly talk I was breathing so fast.

"Hmmm." Bettie looked skeptical but she nodded anyway. "Sure, I can stay late. But check with your mama about any sleepover. Until I hear from her, I expect you back by dark. Got it?"

"Yes, ma'am."

"Don't go getting yourself into trouble and worrying your parents. They've got enough to worry about."

"Okay. Thanks for staying." I headed out the door quickly so Addie wouldn't figure out we were home. She'd know what we were up to and tell Bettie.

We jogged down the road to the Coopers', dodging the puddles forming on the road. The wind blew the stormy clouds quickly across the gray sky.

I couldn't believe they'd arrested Dad. I couldn't believe the zoning passed. I couldn't believe adults didn't care about what was right and wrong. If the sheriff knew Dad was innocent, why had he arrested him? Why wasn't he looking for the person who really did it? The adults had given up and were leaving everything up to us kids. The environment, the truth, our safety. Everything was upside down.

I wished Jeb had never come to town. I wanted everything back the way it used to be. Back when Sophie and I pulled weeds, counted butterfly eggs, and hiked to Paul's Peak for fun. Back when everyone in town got along, and the adults acted like adults, and kids could be kids.

We turned off the road to the Coopers' and followed the path slowly, scanning the ground for tracks. The clouds got darker and let loose hard pelts of rain. Leaves twisted in circles, whispering, "Get out, get out!" I focused on our search and pushed aside thoughts of ghosts and the family graveyard not too far from where we walked.

Something stirred in the underbrush behind us. I spun around and moved the camera up into position. Nothing. I crouched down low with my camera ready. The blood rushed from my face. The rocks sitting at the bottom of my stomach knocked against each other, and my heart thumped in my ears.

Sophie stood still, as pale as I felt. I hadn't thought things all the way through. How would we get away once I got the picture? Squirt him and run? It was a terrible plan, but it was all I had.

We crouched down and moved slowly through the wet underbrush. There was nothing there. We needed to sit and watch like hunters in a deer stand. It'd be safer. Someplace where we could get away if needed, but where we could hide and hopefully not be noticed.

"Let's stake out," I whispered. "Someplace high."

Sophie nodded. "The barn."

"What about the ghost?"

Her eyebrows shot up. Oh, yeah. Right. Sophie didn't believe in ghosts. "Seriously? It was probably the sun reflecting off something. Besides, this whole town is supposedly haunted, but when has a ghost ever attacked anyone?"

She had a good point. I'd been in our store my whole life, and Eloise hadn't attacked me yet … but still. We had to cross the graveyard to get to the barn, and if the ghost of Daryl Cooper had been upset before, he was definitely mad now. "Fine. We'll go to the barn, but you go first."

As I followed her through the woods, my senses were on high alert. Leaves crunched loudly under my feet, wet branches smacked my arms and legs, and rain splattered through the trees in steady rhythm like a horror movie soundtrack. Little drops hit my head and rolled down my back. I felt damp and mushy like a piece of wet moss.

A crow landed above us. It stared down, tilting its head from side to side, and gave out a harsh, "Caw! Caw-caw!" Like it was warning us.

The forest ended at the graveyard. There were a few trees that towered above the long dark shadows of the graves' headstones. The crow left his perch from behind us and flew to the oak in the middle of the graveyard. He let out another, "Caw-caw!"

My heart beat loud and fast. "Let's go around," I whispered. "Not through."

Sophie turned, and we followed the edge of the woods around the outside of the graveyard. The grass around the barn was trimmed and neat, and some of Mrs. Cooper's flowers still bloomed around the side. Jeb's dad would probably have the barn torn down. The flowers would be crushed under the bulldozer. Like our butterfly garden.

We inched our way up through the trees and stopped at the edge of the woods several yards from the barn. I wiped my wet hair out of my eyes and did a quick scan of the area. There was nothing in sight—no wolf, no paw prints, no ghost. Just the loud crow who wouldn't shut up. A few of his crow friends joined him, and they cawed at us and each other. It seemed like a bad omen.

"Did you know a group of crows is called a murder?" Sophie whispered.

"Well, that's comforting." My body tingled again, like it had in the Zaubers' barn right before we saw the Toggle Road Beast.

We dashed across the clearing to the back of the barn and crept along the side. Something bumped loudly inside. Sophie and I froze in place. My instincts told me to run, but I forced myself forward. My feet were bricks. The rocks in my stomach swirled. I moved my camera up into position.

We stopped under the window, and I moved up slowly to peek inside. A black figure floated back and forth in front of the window—the ghost! I fell backward. My stomach lurched. Sophie grabbed my arm, eyes wide.

I heard Jeb's voice, but that couldn't be right. It had to be my imagination. Heart racing, I crawled back to the window and peeked again. Inside, the ghost was gripping Jeb's arm. Everything around Jeb went dark, like I was looking through a long tunnel. The ghost came into sharp focus. It was thick and solid black except for where its face should have been. In its place was a milky white blob. My whole body started trembling.

The ghost gave Jeb's arm a hard squeeze. "Those girls tried to warn you," he said. "This mountain is a spiritual vortex." He leaned down close to Jeb's face. "If you or your dad trespass on this land again, every dead Cooper will *rise* from their graves!" he yelled in a deep, booming voice.

I let my breath out slowly. Okay, it wasn't an actual ghost. It was just a crazy guy in a mask. But that was worse.

Sophie and I ducked down below the window and looked at each other. Her face was white. With shaking hands, I sat down the camera and pulled out my phone to call 911. I didn't have any service. My stomach dropped.

"Dude, you've lost your mind. Let me go!" Jeb yelled.

Thuds, booms, and grunts came from inside.

"Nice try, pretty boy." The guy huffed like he was out of breath. "Let's take a walk."

The barn door flung open. The ghost guy still had Jeb by the arm, pushing him out in front of him. I picked up a rock and threw it as hard as I could. It hit the guy on the side of the head, snapping his head to the side. Jeb pushed back with his body and the guy fell. Jeb tried to run, but the guy grabbed his foot. I was up and running before I could even think. I threw another rock, hitting the guy hard in the chest. He jumped up, pushed me, and grabbed my arm. My wet skin twisted under his fingers. I tried to slip free, but he squeezed harder. Jeb kicked, trying to free himself.

"Run, Sophie!" I yelled. "Get help!"

Something growled behind me. In a flash, soft amber fur brushed against my arm—the wolf! It was on top of the ghost guy, growling and pushing him back through the door of the barn. The guy pulled me and Jeb down with him, and I hit the ground with a hard thud that knocked the wind out of me. The wolf stood on the guy, pinning his shoulders down and snarling inches from his face. Bigger and more menacing than I'd remembered, it filled the air with its hot, sour breath. I fought my arm free, and Jeb kicked until the guy let go of him too.

They guy thrashed his head and body back and forth, knocking off his mask. It was Paul Cooper. "Kids, help me!" he screamed.

Sophie stood completely still, holding my camera with her eyes wide and mouth hanging open. I grabbed her arm and pulled. "Come on, Sophie! We gotta get out of here."

We sprinted through the graveyard to the woods. The branches whipped and splashed against me, stinging my face and arms. We weaved in and out of the trees until we reached the path where we ran faster, leaping over fallen branches and broken rocks until we made it to the road. When we were safely away, I called 911.

"This is Emma Murry. We found Jeb Scott. Paul Cooper had him in the barn at 1222 Black Mountain Road. We ran away. I don't think he followed us." The words shot out in between breaths. I leaned over and put my free hand on my knee, trying to breathe.

"Is anyone injured?"

"Uhh … not really."

"Are you in a safe location?"

"We're walking up the road toward 1225 Black Mountain Road."

"We have officers and an ambulance on the way. Stay on the line until they arrive."

"Okay."

I turned to Jeb and Sophie. "The sheriff's on the way."

Jeb looked at me with wide eyes, and his breath came in short spurts and gasps. "You saved my life!" He grabbed me and gave me a huge hug. I could hear his racing heartbeat and feel his chest rise and fall. Even after all the running and fighting, he still smelled good.

"Break it up, guys!" Sophie said. "We're still sitting ducks here in the road."

Jeb and I stopped hugging.

Sirens blared in the distance and got closer and closer until four cop cars and an ambulance came flying around the corner. The ambulance and one police car stopped when they saw us. The other three sped ahead to the Cooper farm. We sat in the back of the ambulance and dried off as the paramedics cleaned our cuts and checked our arms and legs.

Sheriff Hernandez drove up and stopped his cruiser by the ambulance. Cami and Evelyn came speeding up behind him on their bikes. "We heard bits and pieces on the police scanner," Cami said, dropping her bike and running over to us. "Are you okay?"

I nodded. "We're fine."

"What the heck happened?" Evelyn asked.

I started to tell them, but Jeb jumped in. He said he'd been out looking for us when Paul grabbed him and pulled him into the barn. He made the next part sound way better than it had been, with me bombarding Paul with rocks, and Jeb karate-kicking him. According to Jeb, we had pretty much taken him down when the wolf showed up.

That was a little harder for him to explain, so Sophie chimed in, "It was a red wolf. A really big one, so probably a male. We've seen it before and heard it howling. I got a picture!"

"What?" I yelled, shaking my head. "You were taking pictures instead of running for help?"

"That's why we were out there, right?" asked Sophie. "The whole thing would have been a waste without evidence of the red wolf." She flipped the camera on.

"The whole thing would have been a waste if we were dead!" But I was glad she got a picture. Now we could settle it once and for all. Once she saw it, really stopped and stared at it, there was no way she'd still believe it was a red wolf.

We leaned in to get a better look at the picture on the camera and groaned in disappointment. She'd missed the wolf completely. It was mostly Jeb looking very pale with wide, scared eyes. We could see Paul's hand around his ankle, and in the very corner, there was a tip of a furry tail. The picture was at an angle. Most of it was the floor of the barn.

Cami sighed. "You missed the whole wolf-shifter!"

Sheriff Hernandez gave Cami a side-eye. "Wolf-shifter?"

"Sí, un descendiente de Cuetlachtli. He lives in the woods."

"No, es solo una hisoria. It's made up."

Cami shook her head. "Emma lo vio."

He looked over at me. "What did you see, Emma?"

I pulled out my phone and showed him the paw print. His eyes got wide.

"See?" said Cami. "A wolf-shifter. Like King Cuetlachtli!"

The sheriff took off his hat and wiped the sweat forming on his forehead with the back of his hand. He didn't ask any more questions.

Cami was right. Jeb and I knew what we'd seen—a wolf with Mr. Zauber's amber eyes and pointy, crooked teeth. The same one that tried to chase us out of the barn. But he definitely went after Paul, not us. Mr. Zauber was the wolf-shifter, and he'd saved us.

Chapter 15

Unity: the balance and harmony of all elements.
A unified work looks just right and pleasing to the eye

Early the next morning, my door rattled, waking me out of a nightmare of a guy in a ghost mask squeezing my arms and shaking me. I sat up in the bed, gasping for air.

"Emma, Emma, wake up! Jeb's here!" Addie yelled through my door.

Okay. Good. Not a ghost guy, just Addie.

She banged on the door again.

"Geez. I'm up, thanks."

I took a long drink out of my water bottle and tried to wake up. What would I say to Jeb? My feelings for him were so mixed up. People were complicated. He'd taken a huge risk sneaking around, trying to find the wolf to help clear Dad. It was really nice. Especially since I was ghosting him at the time. But I was still really mad about the ski resort. Sophie and I were going to protest all summer while it was being built.

Mom's butterfly metaphor was so true. Growing up did feel like the stages of a monarch. First, you're a clueless hungry caterpillar. Then, a mixed-up mushy pupa. Then, you slowly emerge into the world, wet, soft, and crumpled, waiting to dry off and straighten out. That was where I was—trying to understand how I could still like Jeb when he didn't value what I valued. I wasn't ready to fly just yet, but I was starting to figure it out.

"He's out front!" Addie yelled.

"Okay, thanks! Now get lost!" I yelled back, looking out my bedroom window.

Jeb stood in the driveway. My stomach flipped and fluttered. My head could tell me to stay away all it wanted, but my heart had a mind of its own.

I changed out of my pajamas, quickly fixed my ponytail, and slid open my window. "Hey!" I yelled.

Jeb looked up. "Hey! I've been trying call you."

"Oh, sorry. I was asleep." Also, his number was still blocked.

"I'm leaving tonight. Do you wanna hike up Paul's Peak before I go?"

I could try one last time to convince him to change his mind. Maybe it wasn't too late. "Sure! Give me a sec."

When I opened my bedroom door, Addie fell into my room. "Go see what he wants!" She hopped up and down in front of me.

"I am! Get lost." She followed me as I ran down the stairs. I opened the front door and popped out, slamming the door behind me. She peeked through the window.

I made a silly face at her and then turned to Jeb. "You're not gonna talk about all the great runs and places to do three-sixties and stuff, are you?"

He smiled. "Nope."

"Good."

I walked next to him down the front stairs and out to the road. The sky was back to its cloudless Carolina periwinkle-blue.

"Is your dad back home?" Jeb asked.

"Yep. They released him last night as soon as Paul confessed to sending the death threat. He was so happy to be cleared and so happy that I was okay that I didn't even get in trouble."

We crossed the road to our usual shortcut by the Zaubers' fence. A soft breeze blew the leaves. They twirled and rustled, dancing to their own beat. Their shadows made a kaleidoscope of light and dark on the ground.

"I knew you were mad after the zoning meeting," Jeb said, "when you didn't answer my texts."

"Yeah, I was. I actually blocked your number." I pulled my phone out to unblock him before I forgot again.

He put his hand on my arm. "My dad drug me away last night before I could tell you why I'd been out looking for you. I wanted to tell you that I've been thinking about everything you've said this week. About butterflies, flowers, wolves, eagles—all that stuff. And I see why it's so important to you."

"You do?"

"Yeah." He let go of my arm and awkwardly rubbed the back of his neck. "Sometimes, I just think about myself. What I want, not what's best for everyone else. You always think of everyone else."

"That's not true."

"It is. All that stuff you said at the zoning meeting about pollinators and how important they are to food and the future. And about beauty—like some stuff is important just because it exists."

"So, you're not buying the Coopers' property?"

"No, we are. Dad's finalizing the sale in town right now."

I stopped walking. The air left my body, and I felt like I was going to cry. "I was hoping you'd change your mind."

"We did. Sort of. Keep walking, I'll show you."

We walked around the circle to the Peak. It still took my breath away, even though I'd seen it hundreds of times. The sunlight made the leaves of the trees glow across the mountains in spotted hues of green. The town sat nestled in the valley below.

"We're not building here," Jeb said.

I turned and looked at him. "What do you mean?"

He had a huge smile. "Dad's buying Wolf Creek Ski Resort. We offered the owner a price he couldn't refuse. We're remodeling the Cooper farmhouse and moving in when it's done. Dad wants to live here."

Wowza. I almost fell over.

"Are you okay?" He laughed.

"Yeah! I'm better than okay."

"You can come to the Peak whenever you want. We're fencing it off, but you can have a key to the gate." He handed me a packet of butterfly weed seeds. "I got these from your store. Your dad said the orange ones are your favorite. Plant these and anything else you want."

Wowza. Wowza. Emotions swirled and twirled inside of me like a skateboard in a perpetual kickflip to heelflip. I started to thank him, but he interrupted.

"That's not all." He reached behind a tree and pulled out a wooden sign. "It's not Paul's Peak anymore," he said, flipping the sign around. "This's *your* peak now."

Painted across the front of the sign in huge block letters was *Emma's Peak*. Whoa.

He pointed to my name on the sign. "Look, it's a super easy anagram. If you take away the apostrophe, it says, *Emma speak*." He looked up into my eyes. "Your speech was so good. You made me see what's important yesterday, and all week, really. It just took it a while to sink in. Now you need to tell the world. We'll start with my three hundred thousand followers."

My head swirled like I flipped three-sixty in a gazelle flip, my insides mastering the most impossible skateboard trick imaginable. Before my brain figured out what I was doing, I reached out and hugged him. He leaned in and hugged me back. It was a great hug full of warmth and friendship. "I'm glad I met you, Jeb," I said.

"I'm glad I met you too, Emma." We stopped hugging, but he kept his arm around me. "That'll be our brand. Emma Speaks." He handed me the sign and snapped our picture. "We'll be an amazing team."

I smiled so big my face hurt.

❦ ❦ ❦

That afternoon, Chester had a celebration lunch at Max's diner. If there were any hurt feelings left over from the zoning meeting, no one showed it. Max even told Sophie he was proud of her speech and said she could go to environmental camp in Sweden next summer if she helped save money by bussing tables two days a week. She was ecstatic.

Then, he made everyone barbeque and gave a couple of bottles of sauce to Chester, hoping to get the word out about his "world-famous" barbeque.

Blair, Matt, and Cole came with two buckets of ice cream—Black Mountain Rocky Road and Peppermint Cream. Mr. and Mrs. Zauber brought several blueberry pies.

Erin sat at a table with Blair, Matt, Cole, and Addie. Commissioner Lightfoot sat with Stella Bearpaw, the mayor, and the mayor's wife. Mr. Zauber gave Chester a hydrangea bush and sat down at the big table in between him and Dad, who was next to Max and across from Dr. Suárez, Sheriff Hernandez, Tía Lupé, and Mom. Sophie, Jeb, Cami, Carlos, Evelyn, and I sat at our own long table. Everyone joked and laughed together as if the zoning meeting had never happened.

Dad stood and held up a glass of Black Mountain Cherry Cream Soda. "I'd like to make a toast to those who solved the case and cleared my name."

Sheriff Hernandez leaned forward and grinned. "Don't thank me, Jimmy. I was only doing my job," he said.

"Not you, Simon. The kids!"

Everyone laughed and picked up their glasses.

"To my daughter Emma and her partners for cracking the case. I'm forever in your debt. And to Simon too, I guess, for arresting Paul and getting him to confess."

"Hear, hear!" everyone said and clinked their glasses together.

"By the way, how did Paul get into our house?" Chester asked as he set his glass down.

"We found the key with the cut-up magazine when we searched his van," Sheriff Hernandez said. "He must've seen Jimmy changing the locks, followed him back to the store, stole the extra key, and bought the postcard and magazine. He used the key later that night to unlock the door and leave the postcard on the table." Sheriff Hernandez held up his glass. "And thanks to Mr. Zauber for holding him in the barn. Otherwise, he might have gotten away."

Everyone turned and looked at Mr. Zauber. "No need to thank me. I happened to be in the right place at the right time. I knew he'd been living in his van in the barn all week, so I was headed over to talk about the next steps—how to fight the zoning—when

I heard yelling and saw the kids running." He smiled at me, and I smiled back. Then I thought he winked. No, I was positive. He definitely winked.

Sheriff Hernandez saw him too. His mouth opened a little and his eyes got wide, but he didn't say anything.

"Paul said he was only trying to scare Jeb," Mr. Zauber added. "He was very adamant that he wasn't actually going to hurt him."

"It didn't seem that way," I said. "He was really mad."

Jeb stood and waved his glass in the air. "I'd like to toast too. Thanks to Emma and Sophie for saving me."

Shouts of "to Emma and Sophie!" and "Hear, hear!" filled the room.

Jeb scooped a huge piece of pie with his fork and held it up. "Also, thank you, pollinators!"

Everyone laughed and clapped. Part of Jeb's love for Black Mountain definitely revolved around food.

When there was nothing left to eat, the kids ditched the party. We went out the back, through the alley, and skated down the side streets to avoid tourists. We cut through the park to the greenway trail and followed it to the butterfly garden.

The afternoon sun was high and bright. It lit up everything around us, making the colors in the garden their most intense shades like a van Gogh.

Sophie was brighter too. She practically glowed. She skated over to the milkweed and jumped off her board. "Let's pull some weeds since we're here."

Evelyn, Cami, Carlos, and I steered over to her and hopped off our boards too.

Jeb tick-tacked in a circle. "Wait, Emma. Show them your ollie, first." He kicked his board over to me. I stopped it with my foot and flipped it up perfectly, catching it in my hand.

"Nice," Jeb said.

"Coolio!" Sophie gave me a thumbs-up.

Jeb cracked up. I did too. Sophie snort-laughed, and then we all lost it. I gave up on the ollie and collapsed in the soft grass. Jeb plopped down next to me, his eyes shining with tears of laughter.

A monarch dried its wings nearby. Its clear shell hung on the milkweed leaf next to it. I grabbed my phone and recorded as its wings opened and closed slowly. It lifted off the flower and fluttered around us before rising higher and higher. I posted the video on our Emma Speaks Insta Story. We already had over one thousand followers.

I thought about what Mom had said again, and she was right. We had all gone through a kind of metamorphosis these past few days. I went from being terrified to speak in public to fighting for what I wanted in front of the whole town, and even though I was disappointed in a lot of people, it was okay. I'd changed the minds of the most important ones. Jeb learned to appreciate things about the environment he hadn't even known mattered a few days ago. And Sophie and I both realized we could expand our best-friend circle and still be BFFs with each other. Change was hard, but it was worth it in the end.

My friends didn't leave when it was time for Mrs. Hartford's art class. I set up my easel so I could see Jeb lying in the meadow with milkweed around him. I painted him—not gray but bright and glowing in the yellow sunlight next to my friends. Behind them in the distance, Emma's Peak soared through the clouds and melted into the sky. The art elements I'd been studying all week—color, value, form, and line—balanced together perfectly for my last term: *unity*.

Acknowledgments

This book would not have come together without the time, help, and support of so many others. I'm very thankful for:
- The people of Black Mountain, North Carolina, who are always terrific hosts when they showcase the beauty of their mountains, garden, and greenway;
- The Georgetown College community, especially Dr. Gwen Curry and the ladies of Kappa Delta;
- The English department at UNC Charlotte, especially Bryn Chancellor, Dr. Mark West, and Dr. Elizabeth Gargano;
- My amazing beta readers, Jeni Chappelle, Maria Linn, and Lori Keckler, and SCBWI Carolinas and WriteMentor critique groups for their insights, thoughtful feedback, and encouragement;
- Lori Keckler for sharing the Aztec legend of Cuetlachtli and proofing all the Spanish, and Jessica Jacks-Turkas for hashing out the plot over our morning coffee meet-ups;
- Cody, Lilly, Ollie Bear, and Riley—the best doggy friends a human could have—and their woodsy walks, couch

snuggles, and reminding me that every good book needs at least one spaniel;
- My dad and mom, who instilled in me a love of nature and a love of books;
- Mikaela, Carleigh, Gracie, and Jacob, who are my cheerleaders and sounding boards, and who are the creators, nature lovers, and world-changers that inspired the characters in this book;
- Gracie for bringing the chapter heading illustrations to life in such a unique and creative way and for being willing to attempt anything, always with a smile;
- And everyone at Warren Publishing for their creative input and hard work.
- Finally, thanks to Steve, without whose unconditional love and support none of this would be possible.

Author Bio

REBECCA LAXTON has served school communities as an afterschool program director, teacher, reading specialist, and school psychologist. While working for Boone County Schools, she was named the Kentucky School Psychologist of the Year for collaborating with teachers and administrators to write and evaluate an emotional intelligence curriculum.  She attended Georgetown College, Eastern Kentucky University, and, most recently, the University of North Carolina at Charlotte, earning an MLS with a concentration in creative writing and children's literature. Currently, she is a dyslexia practitioner with Braintrust and lives in North Carolina with her husband Steve, four kids, and three very cute, extremely spoiled dogs. Rebecca invites you to visit her online at rebeccalaxton.com.

Illustrator Bio

GRACIE LAXTON is a freelance graphic designer and dance choreographer from North Carolina but is currently based in New York City. A 2021 graduate of Central Academy of Technology and Arts in Monroe, North Carolina, she attends Marymount Manhattan College, pursuing degrees in dance and art.

www.ingramcontent.com/pod-product-compliance
Lightning Source LLC
LaVergne TN
LVHW050551281224
799992LV00013B/513